DANGER FROM SPACE

Jay B. Greene

Boketon Press

Copyright © 2024 by Jay B. Greene
All rights reserved. This book or any portion thereof may
not be reproduced or used in any manner whatsoever
without the express written permission of the publisher,
except for the use of brief quotations in a book review.

ISBN (Paperback): 979-8-9902256-4-0
ISBN (eBook): 979-8-9902256-5-7

Cover Design by Adam Hay Studio, UK
Interior Formatting by Steve Mead Graphic Design

Printed in the United States of America
This book is a work of fiction. Names, characters,
businesses, events, and incidents are products of the
author's imagination or used fictitiously. Any resemblance
to actual persons, living or dead, is purely coincidental.

In memory of the late Arthur C. Clarke, Isaac
Asimov and Ray Bradbury—science fiction writer
visionaries who, during my teenage years, ignited my
imagination and taught me to dream without limits.

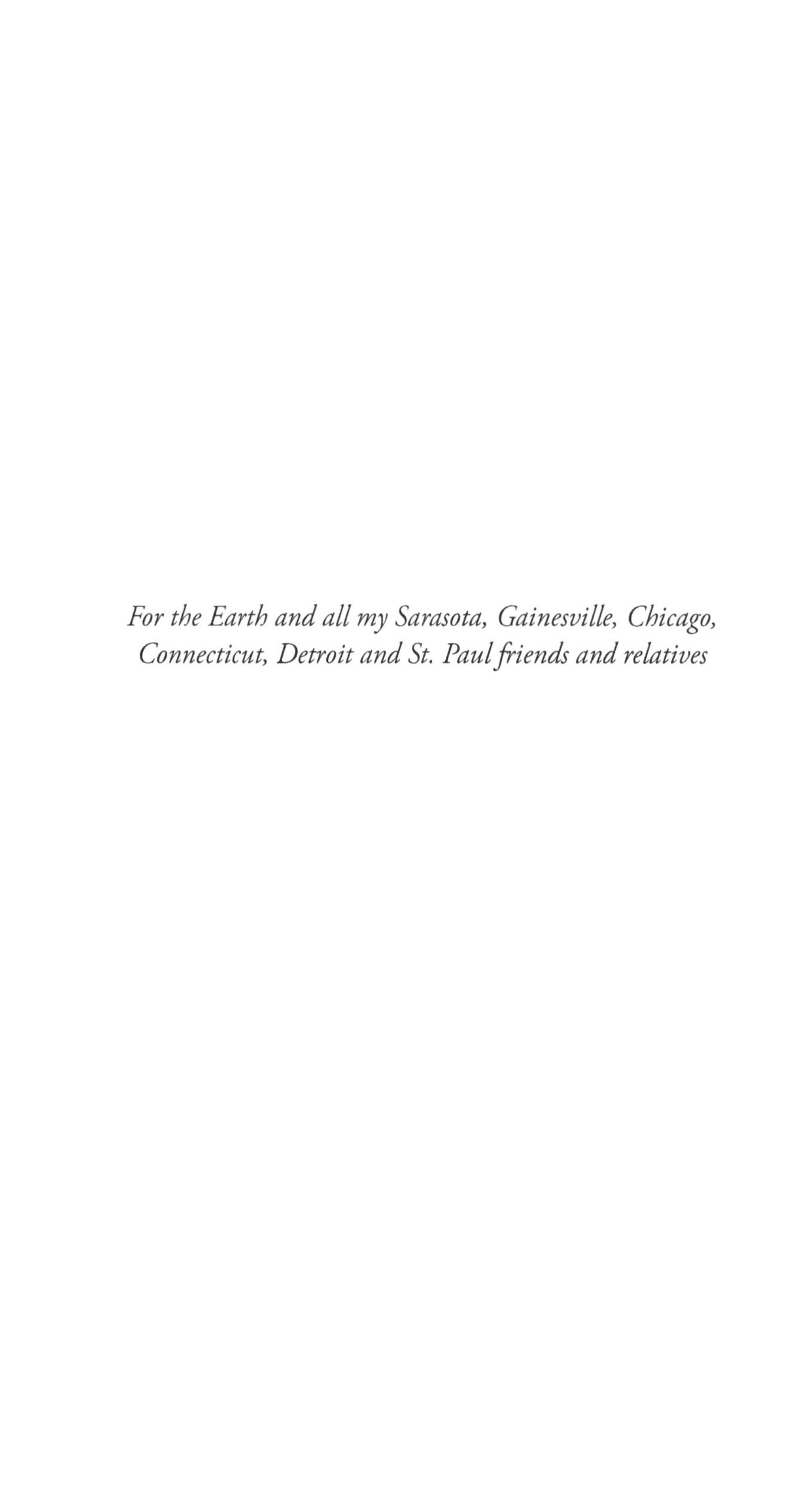

*For the Earth and all my Sarasota, Gainesville, Chicago,
Connecticut, Detroit and St. Paul friends and relatives*

CONTENTS

CAMP WAYBEGONE

July 2063

For nine-year-old Tim Smith, the annual summer camp in the Blue Ridge Mountains of North Carolina was a cherished tradition. Nestled among tall pine trees and rocky creeks, Camp Waybegone was a place of adventure and camaraderie, contrasting sharply with the changing planet and the extraordinary events that were about to unfold.

This was Tim's third summer at the camp, and he had already made a name for himself among the campers and counselors. With 12 merit badges and three pothole medals, Tim was an accomplished camper, even outshining many of the older kids. His best summer friend, George Clarke, was his constant companion; together, they were an unbeatable duo.

Little did Tim know that his previous accomplishments at camp would pale compared to the mysterious encounter he was about to have this particular summer.

One bright afternoon, the campers set out on a hike. Tim's group, Cabin 12, was joined by the younger Cabin 15 group of 7 and 8-year-olds and the Cabin 4 group of

11 and 12-year-olds.

Tim's attention was suddenly drawn to a flash of light in the woods. Ignoring the calls of his friend George and counselor Stephen Martin, he ran away from the group, his actions uncharacteristically impulsive.

"Tim, where are you going?" George yelled as Tim bolted away.

Stephen, an athletic 19-year-old counselor with a protective nature, immediately chased after Tim, with George following closely behind.

"Tim, come back," shouted Stephen.

They found Tim standing in a small clearing, clutching a shiny rock.

Suddenly, Stephen saw a burst of light, a puff of purple gas and dust spraying around Tim.

"Drop it, Tim, and stand back," Stephen said as he waved his arms. "It might be dangerous."

But Tim couldn't help himself. He seemed entranced, his gaze fixed on the rock as it crumbled in his hands. It released a sweet-smelling vapor. The gas and dust swirled around him, and Tim inhaled deeply, unable to resist.

A curious smile crossed his lips. He began to glow with a kaleidoscope of colors. The vibrant hues danced across his skin, mesmerizing Stephen and George and filling them with awe.

The gas and dust penetrated him. The substances made him feel lightheaded and gave him a jolt of energy.

"What's happening?" Stephen shouted out as a wave of energy passed through him.

George, who was further away from Tim than Stephen, also sensed an energy coming from the gas and dust. He looked at his friend with worry. "Tim, say something. You look ... different."

As the rock disintegrated, the colorful glow faded, leaving behind a light mist and fine powder on Tim's hand and arm.

"Tim, are you all right?" asked a shaken Stephen.

Without a word, Tim collapsed to the ground.

Stephen and George rushed to his side.

Tim was unconscious, breathing heavily, but his fingers were moving up and down very quickly.

"What is this?" Stephen said. "I feel strange."

"It's that purple gas," George said. "It knocked Tim out."

"He's breathing at least," Stephen said.

They stood beside Tim. His eyes were closed, but his fingers continued to flutter.

"What's he doing with his fingers?" George asked.

"I don't know, but we've got to get him to the infirmary," Stephen said. "George, do you remember the way back to the trail?"

"Of course," George replied, slightly offended. "I'm a Pathfinder class 3."

"I'll carry Tim, but I want you to gather the group and lead them back to the camp. Then I want you to go to the infirmary, tell Nurse Paula what happened and tell her to be ready."

"Is Tim going to be all right?"

"I don't know. We need to get him help. Can you make it?" Stephen asked, his voice steady with determination.

"Sure," George said.

"Then go," Stephen said.

George and sprinted back toward the main trail. He told the group it was an emergency, that Stephen was helping Tim, and that they should follow him back to camp.

Stephen picked Tim up without any problems. A former high school football player and weightlifter, Stephen carried Tim as easily as if he were a baby. He ran back the three miles to the camp infirmary in record time.

When Stephen arrived, George was already there, and Paula was ready.

"Nurse Paula, Tim is unconscious. We've got to wake him up," Stephen exclaimed excitedly.

"Bring him in here. On the table," said Paula as she pointed to the examination room.

"George told me about the rock, dust, and gas," she said. "What happened?"

"I don't know exactly. Tim just ran off from the group. I chased after him. When I got to the clearing, I saw him holding this rock. It crumbled into dust, and this gas surrounded him. He looked at me with a surprised look on his face, and then he collapsed," said Stephen.

Paula listened to Tim's heartbeat with a stethoscope. It was high but steady.

"He has this powder on his hand and arm. I have some, too. What is it?" Stephen said.

"I'm not sure. Let me look," she said.

As Tim lay on the table, still unconscious, Paula looked over him and saw the purple dust. She noticed some was on Stephen.

"How do you feel?" Paula asked.

"Great. Never better," Stephen said.

"Good. I will get to you next," Paula said. "I see this purple powder on Tim's hand. It is much thicker than yours. You said Tim inhaled the gas? Did you inhale it, too?"

"Yes, a little. George did, too, when we ran up to Tim. It was all around Tim, and then it vanished," Stephen said.

"How did you feel when you inhaled it?"

"I got dizzy, weak, and then a few seconds later, I got a jolt of energy. Tim must have gotten too much. He was knocked out," Stephen said.

Paula turned to George. "How do you feel?"

"Okay, I inhaled a little of the gas. Not too much. Like Stephen, I was dizzy and then returned with the other kids. They were way more tired than me when we got to camp," George said.

"We can be thankful you didn't have any dust on you like Tim and Stephen," Paula said. "Why don't you go back to the cabin and rest? I will see you later with the doctor."

"Do I have to? I want to stay with Tim!" George said.

"All right, but just sit in the chair and be quiet," Paula said. "I need to take Tim's pulse."

As she was doing that, Tim opened his eyes.

"Hey, Tim, glad to see you. How do you feel?" Paula asked with a smile.

"All right, I suppose. I'm a little tired," said Tim as he opened his eyes.

"You have some purple dust on your arms and face, a little on your shirt," said Paula as she wiped the powder off Tim with a moist paper towel. "Here's a camp shirt. Put this on and give me yours."

"All right, if I have to," said Tim as he took off his light blue T-shirt.

Paula put the shirt and paper towel covered in the dust in a plastic bag and marked it. "I want to save this for the doctor," she said.

"What doctor?" said Tim.

"You'll see. How do you feel?" she asked again.

"I tell you, I'm all right," he said, feeling irritated.

"Open your eyes. I want to take a look at your pupils," she asked.

Paula took a close look with a penlight. She was surprised at the color of his eyes. Once a clear light blue, as she remembered, his eyes had shifted to a unique color, a darker shade of purple and blue.

"Can you see me clearly?" she asked Tim.

"Everything looks a little blurry now that you mention it," he said.

"Don't you have blue eyes?" Paula asked, scanning his face for signs of distress.

"I think so," Tim said.

"You feel tired, a little warm and your eyes are blurry. Anything else?" asked Paula, trying to understand his symptoms better.

"Yes. Why is my heart beating so fast?" asked Tim.

"I don't know. Something happened when you picked up that rock and inhaled that gas," said Paula, perplexed by Tim's symptoms.

Based on what she saw, whatever Tim had inhaled was not life-threatening, but it was beyond her expertise.

"I'm going to call my doctor friend to have him take a look at you. Just close your eyes and rest," she said.

"All right, but I don't remember picking up any rock," Tim said matter-of-factly.

Upon hearing this, Paula asked, "What was the last thing you remember?"

"I was running in the woods. That's all," he said.

"Just lay there and rest. I want to look at Stephen," said Paula.

Paula turned to Stephen. "Let me take your pulse, then I'll take your temperature. When the doctor gets here, I want him to look at you, too," she said as she wiped off Stephen's dust, put it in a plastic bag and marked it.

"Your pulse is high at 100 beats per minute. It seems high for you," she asked.

"Well, I did run three miles with Tim," Stephen said.

"Your temperature also is a little high at 101," Paula said.

"Am I going to be all right?" Stephen asked.

"Yes, Tim's pulse and temperature are higher than yours, and he seems to be handling it all right. I want to monitor you both until the doctor arrives," Paula said.

She looked over to Tim, who had fallen asleep. His vital signs were elevated, but he seemed to be resting quietly. Whatever he inhaled wasn't putting his life in danger.

"I'm going to call Dr. Ledbetter and see if he can come over and look you all over," said Paula with concern. "This is beyond me."

More than ten years before, Paula had met Dr. Charles Ledbetter, a neurologist and toxicology specialist at the

University of North Carolina Asheville Medical Center, through her late husband, John, who had died seven years earlier in a mountain climbing accident.

The two medical professionals had gone through a lot. They had grown closer since Sonya, Charles' wife, had died of breast cancer the year before.

When Dr. Ledbetter got Paula's message after his morning classes, he canceled his appointments and arrived later that afternoon.

In addition to wanting to help his friend, his curiosity was piqued by Paula's account of the purple dust that seemed to have caused Tim's collapse and how his eyes had changed from blue to purplish blue.

By the time Dr. Ledbetter arrived two hours later, Tim had awakened. His eyes were bright and alert, and he was ravenously hungry.

"How do you feel, Tim?" Dr. Ledbetter asked.

"I feel fine. Why is everybody asking me that?" he asked.

"I understand you had a close encounter with a strange rock in the woods and passed out. One of your friends had to carry you back to camp," Dr. Ledbetter said.

"I don't remember anything like that," Tim said.

"Oh? Well, let's take a look at you," the doctor said.

Dr. Ledbetter examined Tim thoroughly, taking blood and saliva samples. Despite the strange circumstances, Tim appeared remarkably healthy. His pulse, blood pressure and temperature were all regular.

"Do you mind if I take a look at your eyes?" Dr. Ledbetter asked as he removed an eye otoscope from his medical bag.

"My eyes aren't blurry anymore," Tim said. "What do you see?"

"Hmm. Your eyes seem normal," said the doctor. "Paula says they changed color to a purplish blue. Is that your normal eye color?"

"Let me see," Tim said.

Paula brought him a hand mirror. When Tim saw his eyes, he exclaimed, "My eyes changed? How?"

"That's what I'd like to find out, among other things," Dr. Ledbetter said.

"Charles, are you going to test this dust?" Paula asked. "Tim says he feels fine now, but you heard what George and Stephen said about how he glowed and collapsed once exposed."

Tim looked worried and started to get confused. "If you test this sample at the Medical Center lab, will you tell me what you find?"

"How did you know I want to take it to the medical center's lab?" a surprised Dr. Ledbetter asked.

"Just promise me you will tell me what you find," Tim said.

"Paula, I am glad you took these samples from Tim and Stephen. I have a geologist friend whom I want to consult as well. I never heard of a rock behaving like this," Dr. Ledbetter said.

"Just don't tell anyone," Tim said again.

"Of course," Dr. Ledbetter said.

"I will tell you, your parents and Paula what I find. By the way, Paula must tell your parents what happened to you in the woods. I will recommend they monitor you closely at home with your family doctor," he said.

"I know," Tim said. "But I want you to promise me you won't reveal to anybody what happened to me."

Dr. Ledbetter smiled. "Don't worry." He thought something had happened to this intelligent boy when he was exposed to the strange properties of the rock, dust and gas.

"I promise to keep your secret," said Dr. Ledbetter, adding: "Tim, can I have your permission to do confidential tests on the dust and blood? Whatever we find, I will not reveal your name or that you were exposed to the dust. How does that sound?"

"That sounds all right," Tim said.

"You can trust us. Once the tests are done, we will contact you to discuss the results with your parents, of course," he said.

Tim didn't reply. During the conversation between Dr. Ledbetter and Paula, Tim heard voices coming from the present and the future. He didn't understand.

CHAPTER 1:
THE COSMIC REVELATION

Kennedy Space Center, 11 a.m., May 1, 2078

Tim Smith, a 23-year-old NASA prodigy, leaned forward in his seat, eyes fixed on the screen displaying the James Webb Space Telescope feed. He had directed the powerful instrument to focus on a seemingly unremarkable patch of space outside Pluto in the Kuiper belt, a distant region beyond Neptune, over 2.6 billion miles from Earth.

Based on a vision, Tim suspected the event was starting to unfold. Suddenly, it happened. An imperfection in starlight, a slight wavelength bending, confirmed his vision: a wormhole had opened.

His heart raced as the telescope's sensors picked up something more astonishing. The data show infrared light and the unmistakable signature of heat energy.

Tim double-checked to ensure the computer collected the data on what he was witnessing. There was no doubt. An advanced hybrid fusion-antimatter engine had ignited. As he had predicted months earlier, a massive spacecraft from another world was hurtling toward Earth.

As he calculated the spacecraft's distance, trajectory,

and speed, even Tim was astonished: the spacecraft was heading straight for Earth at 72 million mph and would arrive in less than 30 days.

Tim's pulse quickened as the reality of what he had just proved set in. He had little time to complete implementing his plan from six months earlier. But it was the only chance for Earth to prepare for what was coming.

Taking a deep breath, Tim lifted his arm to speak into his wristphone. "Peggy, come quickly and bring your father. You've got to see this."

"What is it?" Peggy asked.

"I've found it. Come," Tim said.

Five minutes later, Peggy and her father, Dr. Leonard Bouchard, a former astronaut and NASA engineer, arrived at Tim's lab.

The room was dimly lit, and the glow from the monitors cast a blue hue across their faces. Tim had a serious expression, and his eyes were fixed on the data streaming across the screens.

"Tim, what's going on?" asked Peggy, her tone a mix of curiosity and concern.

Tim didn't look up. "I've confirmed a wormhole opening at the inner edge of the Kuiper belt," he said, rapidly tapping his fingers on the keyboard.

"But that's not all. There's a spacecraft—massive— using advanced fusion-antimatter propulsion. It's headed straight for Earth, and it's moving fast. We have 30 days."

Leonard leaned closer to the screen. "Are you sure about the fusion signature?" he asked, his voice calm but intense.

Tim nodded, finally turning to face them. "Positive. The infrared spectrum and heat emission patterns are unmistakable. This isn't just a probe or a piece of debris. It's a fully operational ship and not from around here."

Peggy glanced at her father before stepping forward. "What's the trajectory? Can we trace it back to its origin?"

"I'm not sure. That's what I'm working on now," Tim replied, his focus returning to the monitors. "I've got data on the wormhole, but it opened and closed within two seconds. We might need a different program to locate the same gravitational distortion at the originating coordinate."

"Did you sense anything," asked Peggy, knowing Tim's special psychic powers.

"Yes, I got a flash of intelligent life. I'm trying to lock down the gravitational wave signature from the data we collected when the wormhole opened. If we can figure out where it came from, we might be able to determine who— or what—is on board."

Leonard crossed his arms, deep in thought. "This could be first contact, or it could be something far more dangerous. We must inform NASA immediately and prepare for every possible scenario."

"I've already sent the preliminary data to NASA," Tim said, typing a final command into his computer.

"You should talk with Space Force and brief them through NASA channels," Tim said.

"Roger, the White House should also be notified," Leonard said.

"You know the protocol better than me, sir," Tim replied. "Tell them we should assume this first contact could be hostile. I got a sense something is wrong on that ship."

Peggy placed a hand on Tim's shoulder, her voice steady but laced with urgency. "We'll figure this out. Did you get any data on the ship?"

"Just the fusion engine when it ignited. I am tracking it now, and it is gaining speed. I'll need your help, Peggy, to do the calculations, but it must be massive," Tim said.

"If it is picking up speed, it may arrive sooner than 30 days. We need to move fast. There's no telling what's on that ship—or what it wants," Peggy said.

Tim nodded, his mind racing with the possibilities. "This danger from space is what I told you both about last year."

"I didn't want to believe your theory about a spaceship coming to Earth," said Leonard. "Now it looks like you were right."

"Thanks for having faith in Tim, Dad," Peggy said. "You went on a limb to persuade NASA to allow Tim to use the JWST."

"It wasn't just me. Tim gained credibility with NASA after Terra Nova," Leonard said.

Tim's voice was calm. "Sir, there is no doubt in my mind this spacecraft comes from Terra Nova," he said, his eyes locked on the computer screen.

"It certainly looks that way, but can you prove it?" asked Leonard.

"I'm going to try," Tim said.

"We never doubted you, Tim," said Peggy.

The implications of their words hung heavy in the air.

Terra Nova was a distant exoplanet harboring life Tim had discovered six months earlier. NASA assigned a team to study what lifeforms might exist on the planet, but no one expected contact to happen so suddenly or close to home.

"Honestly, I wasn't completely sure until we could prove it with data," Tim said.

"NASA will need to look at what we have very closely," Leonard said. "I don't see how they can come to any other conclusion. We will soon have first contact."

<hr>

The interior of the alien spacecraft was shrouded in an unnatural stillness, the kind that only deep space can bring. The corridors were dimly lit by a soft, bluish light emanating from the walls, casting long shadows that danced eerily with the ship's subtle movements.

The air was thick with an otherworldly quiet, broken only by the occasional soft beeping of control panels and the low hum of the ship's systems.

Rows of sleek, cylindrical transport chambers lined the walls, each meticulously sealed and softly illuminated. The chambers were opaque, hiding their contents from view. Still, a faint glow pulsed within, suggesting life—or something akin to it—lay dormant inside.

Artificial intelligence robots glided silently through the ship's corridors, their movements smooth and purposeful. These machines were unlike anything seen on Earth—sleek, angular, and distinctly alien, with glowing eyes that flickered with intelligence.

Their metallic bodies emitted a soft, almost musical, series of beeps and clicks as they communicated in a language of pure data, a symphony of alien sounds that echoed through the ship's interior.

The robots tended to the ship's systems, checking the status of the sleep pods and monitoring the ship's complex operations. Occasionally, one of them would pause, its glowing blue eyes narrowing as it processed new information before resuming its duties.

Despite the ship's relative calm, there was a sense of immense power within its walls, a latent energy that could be unleashed at any moment. The ship was a marvel of alien engineering, designed for a purpose unknown to those on Earth.

But one thing was sure: whatever—or whoever—was on board was now on a direct course for Earth, and their intentions would soon be revealed.

As the spacecraft hurtled through the cold expanse of deep space, its destination drew nearer, and the beeping sounds of the ship's systems quickened as if in anticipation of what was to come.

Tim sensed the alien spacecraft drawing nearer. He looked at the clock on the wall. It was ticking down to a moment of unprecedented contact.

"Peggy, time to alert the others," Tim said.

CHAPTER 2:
PEGGY

2071-2074

Tim met Peggy in Gainesville at the University of Florida during the fall semester of their freshman year. Peggy caught Tim's eye during an 8 a.m. survey course on 20th and 21st-century U.S. history.

She caught *everyone's* eye.

Each morning, Peggy sauntered into the lecture hall a few minutes after class started, her blonde, wavy hair disheveled. She carried a backpack over one arm and walked fast, almost sideways, to any open chair.

Tim was captivated by Peggy from the moment he saw her. Her hurried entrances and casual yet effortlessly natural and beautiful appearance made her stand out in the crowded lecture hall.

He knew he had to meet her but needed a plan.

After admiring her from afar for several days, Tim decided to act. He noticed that Peggy always arrived just a few minutes late, so he started arriving early to class to ensure he could sit near an open seat.

On Friday morning, Tim saw his chance when Peggy arrived as usual, scanning the room for a place to sit. Tim had deliberately chosen a seat with an empty chair beside it. When Peggy spotted it, she quickly made her way over.

As she settled in, Tim leaned over and said with a friendly smile, "Running late again? Don't worry, I saved you a seat." Peggy, slightly embarrassed but grateful, smiled back.

After class, Tim walked out with her, and they talked about their mutual dislike for history so early in the morning. Tim's easygoing nature made it easy for Peggy to open up.

She told him her father was an engineer at NASA, and she was leaning toward majoring in a space science program. She didn't know which one. Tim told her he had chosen astrophysics.

From that day on, they sat together in every class they could arrange. They began studying with several friends they met at UF or knew from high school.

Tim was from Sarasota, a coastal city on Florida's Gulf Coast, and Peggy was from Cocoa, a town with a rich history tied to space exploration.

A decade earlier, NASA had been forced to relocate from Merritt Island and Cape Canaveral to Cocoa due to the rising Atlantic Ocean driven by climate change.

Tim often shared stories about the changes that had affected Sarasota, particularly noting how the sunsets had shifted from vibrant oranges to deeper reds. Meanwhile, Peggy recounted how Cocoa became the center of activity following NASA's move inland. Their shared experiences of Florida's changing landscape and mutual passion for science brought them closer together.

However, Tim and Peggy's discussions weren't always

about classes or the heavy environmental issues on everyone's minds, especially college students who would be expected to deal with increasingly complex challenges as they entered the workforce.

After weeks of casual conversations and shared interests, Tim finally mustered the courage to ask Peggy out on a dinner date.

Wanting to make it memorable, he carefully chose a unique restaurant that reflected their love for adventure and shared a connection to Florida's natural beauty.

Tim picked out a charming, eco-friendly cafe in a secluded corner of Gainesville. The restaurant, known as "The Greenhouse," was famous for its organic, locally sourced cuisine and environmental commitment.

The building was a marvel of green architecture, with walls of glass that allowed diners to feel as if they were eating in the middle of a lush garden. The interior was filled with thriving plants, soft lighting, and warm wood accents, creating an atmosphere that was both intimate and in harmony with nature.

The menu was of carefully curated dishes highlighting Florida's diverse culinary heritage. It included fresh seafood from the Gulf, seasonal vegetables, and citrus-infused desserts.

Knowing Peggy's love for seafood, Tim recommended the grilled snapper with zesty mango salsa and roasted sweet potatoes.

As they dined, the conversation flowed effortlessly. While they touched on the subjects that had brought them together—science, exploration, and the environment— Tim steered the discussion toward lighter topics.

They laughed about their early mornings in the American history class, where they first met and shared stories from their childhoods in Sarasota and Cocoa.

The dinner was filled with tasty, meaningful conversation and a growing connection. By the time they left The Greenhouse, Tim and Peggy knew this was just the beginning of something special.

Tim and Peggy's love blossomed during their undergraduate years. An insatiable curiosity about the universe drove them, and their shared passion for science and exploration laid a strong foundation for their relationship.

One memorable moment occurred during a camping trip to St. George Island in late November during their senior year. They had set up their tent under a clear, star-studded sky, planning to stargaze through the night.

As they lay on a blanket, Peggy pointed out constellations while Tim recited scientific facts about each star in his typically analytical way.

"Okay, Mr. Scientist, enough with the facts. Let's see if you can make up a constellation story. How about that cluster over there?" said Peggy, giggling.

"All right, that cluster ... let's call it 'The Lost Socks.' It's the mythical place where all our missing socks go after we do laundry," said Tim, trying to maintain a straight face.

"And what's the legend behind it?" she said with a short laugh.

"Legend has it that the sock overlord, who controls all

missing socks, lives there. He's got an entire kingdom full of unmatched socks, and he likes to wear them as crowns," Tim said.

"Well, the next time I lose a sock, I'll blame it on the sock overlord," Peggy said.

They both burst into laughter, the kind that left them gasping for breath and leaving them feeling light and carefree under the vast sky.

Their love deepened through quiet, intimate moments, often during late-night discussions about the universe.

One evening, after an exhausting day of school and lab classes, they found themselves on the roof of Tim's dorm building, lying on an old mattress, looking up at the stars.

"Do you ever think about how small we are compared to all this? It's humbling, isn't it?" said Peggy softly.

"Yeah, it is. But it's also comforting in a way. Knowing that we're part of something so much bigger," said Tim, nodding.

They lay in silence, the night air cool and comforting. Peggy turned her head to look at Tim, her eyes reflecting the starlight.

"I'm glad we're exploring it together, Tim. The universe, life ... everything. I can't imagine doing it with anyone else," Peggy said.

"Neither can I, Peg. You've been my best discovery," said Tim.

His voice was deep and sincere, and Peggy felt a warmth spread through her. In moments like these, they both realized the depth of their love for each other. It wasn't just about their shared interests or the excitement of discovery but their quiet understanding and companionship.

Despite their intense bond, an unspoken tension lingered between them. Tim had never shared with Peggy his mysterious encounter as a child at Camp Waybegone, where he discovered a space rock that granted him special powers.

Even though Peggy suspected something, he kept this secret buried, partly out of fear of being misunderstood and partly out of a desire to protect Peggy from the unknown. He didn't want the mystery to overwhelm their relationship.

One evening, after an exhausting day of school and lab classes, they found themselves again on the roof of Tim's dorm building, sitting on beach lounge chairs, looking up at the stars.

"You seem far away. What's on your mind?" asked Peggy.

Before responding, Tim hesitated. "Just ... just thinking about how much we don't know. There's something ...."

"You know you can tell me anything, right? Whatever it is, we'll face it together," Peggy said.

Tim looked at her, his heart heavy with the weight of his secret. He reached out and held her hand, squeezing it gently.

"I know. And someday, I will. Just ... not yet."

Peggy nodded, sensing the depth of his struggle. She didn't push him, respecting his boundaries, but she hoped he would trust her enough to one day share the secret she felt he had.

Their relationship was a beautiful blend of shared passions, laughter, and unspoken understanding. They were partners in every sense, navigating the complexities of life, college, and the mysteries of the universe together.

CHAPTER 3:
THE SCHOLAR WITH A SECRET

University of Florida, 2075

Tim's encounter with the space rock at Camp Waybegone was a life-altering moment that dramatically and profoundly transformed him.

The encounter had given him extraordinary extrasensory powers and abilities—precognition, clairvoyance, telepathy and remote viewing—that set him apart from normal humans.

While difficult at first, Tim gradually gained control over his psychic abilities. By concentrating his mind, he could foresee the future and anticipate dangers.

He was cautious in using his powers and aware of the possible repercussions because there were times when he would lose consciousness or experience anxiety attacks.

Nevertheless, there were instances when unexpected thoughts or stimuli caught him off guard, especially during nighttime dreams when he could not control the visions.

Only a few people knew the story of the space rock and Tim's abilities: George Clarke, Stephen Martin, Dr.

Charles Ledbetter, Paula Winters, and Tim's parents, Gale and Clara.

Although Dr. Ledbetter announced the discovery of newvidium to the world in 2064—a year after researching the exotic dust from the space rock—he did not reveal that the new element had given Tim, and to a lesser extent, Stephen, extraordinary ESP abilities. The others also honored Tim's request to keep the secret.

Tim's mother, Clara, a deeply religious woman, believed the space rock was a gift from a higher power that protected her son and was deposited on Earth from the heavens to save it somehow.

She encouraged Tim to use his powers wisely, hoping he and everyone would understand the space rock's purpose one day.

But now, days before Tim and Peggy's wedding, Tim faced the decision of whether to tell Peggy the story about the space rock and his superpowers.

Even though he knew she would accept it without question, he was torn between his love for her and the need to protect her. He was always on edge, thinking that his secret would become public and someone would get hurt.

Early on, his father warned him that revealing his abilities could attract unwanted attention and that he needed to keep his special powers a secret.

Although they didn't tell Tim their deepest fears, his parents worried their son might be kidnapped and exploited for sinister plots, such as being forced to use his abilities for criminal activities or being held for ransom.

On the other hand, telling her could help him protect

his secret. Even after 12 years of practice, he was still learning how to use his abilities efficiently. He was sure she could help him fully unravel the mystery and take care of him when he overused his powers.

Tim's internal struggle over his secret was compounded by his deep respect for Peggy's father, Dr. Leonard Bouchard. If he told Peggy, he certainly would need to tell her father.

The NASA scientist and former astronaut first encountered Tim while an undergraduate at UF. Tim had been dating Peggy, and she had frequently shared stories of Tim's remarkable scientific insights and his ability to think outside the conventional bounds of astrophysics.

Intrigued, Leonard arranged to meet Tim during one of his visits to see Peggy. Over a dinner that quickly turned into a deep and engaging discussion about the mysteries of the universe, Leonard was impressed by Tim's profound understanding of complex astrophysical concepts.

Dr. Bouchard had been a mentor to many young scientists, but he saw something uniquely special in Tim. He was especially impressed by the young man's extraordinary intellect, keen curiosity, astonishing insight, and natural charisma. What stood out even more was Tim's ability to explain these ideas with clarity and passion.

Recognizing Tim's potential, Leonard decided to take him under his wing. He invited Tim to attend NASA seminars as his guest and introduced him to important figures within the agency. Leonard viewed Tim as a brilliant scientist and a leader capable of inspiring others and driving innovation. He was especially impressed by Tim's unique abilities.

His guidance was instrumental in helping Tim secure an internship at NASA, where he quickly distinguished himself with his innovative approaches and uncanny ability to foresee and mitigate potential issues.

Leonard could see that Tim's mind worked at a rare level, even among NASA's brightest minds. His groundbreaking research on exoplanet detection and innovative approach to solving complex cosmic puzzles caught the agency's attention.

When Tim graduated with top honors in astrophysics from UF, NASA immediately offered him a full-time position, which he eagerly accepted.

CHAPTER 4:
LIFE AMONG THE STARS

Titusville, Summer 2076

For Tim, working at NASA was not just a job but a gateway to a career that would allow the young scientist to fully harness his unique abilities.

Tim's hiring was marked by excitement that reverberated through NASA's corridors. Senior scientists and engineers were eager to see what this young prodigy would bring to the team.

During Tim's first year at NASA, Leonard became a source of wisdom and encouragement. He marveled how Tim's unique abilities became invaluable assets in NASA's most ambitious projects.

After rotating through several departments during his first summer, Tim asked to be assigned to NASA's Search for Extraterrestrial Intelligence project.

He wanted to prove his vision that a perfect Goldilocks planet existed not far from Earth in the Milky Way. He also sensed that this exoplanet had intelligent lifeforms. He just needed a little time to discover the truth of his profound space visions.

Named after the fairy tale character Goldilocks, who

found things "just right," a Goldilocks planet was thought to be in a zone around a sun whose temperature allowed water to exist.

NASA's search for these planets, also known as exoplanets, began in the 1970s. Tens of thousands have been identified since 1992, but only a few were found to be in a "habitable zone."

Tim, who quickly established himself as a brilliant astrophysicist, joined a team of passionate scientists dedicated to identifying exoplanets in the habitable zones of distant stars.

He was also thrilled that Peggy was hired as an astrophysicist to join the SETI program, although initially in a different team than Tim.

Now part of NASA, Tim and Peggy settled into life outside of work in Titusville, a small town north of Cocoa near the Kennedy Space Center. Their home was filled with computers, books, star maps, and telescopes, reflecting their shared interests.

Despite their busy schedules, Tim and Peggy managed to carve out time for each other. They shared quiet dinners, stargazing sessions, and lengthy discussions about the universe's mysteries while listening to classical music.

As the daughter of Leonard Bouchard, one of the pioneering astronauts who journeyed to Mars a decade earlier, Peggy had a significant legacy to uphold.

During her first year at NASA, Peggy contributed to SETI by developing advanced signal detection algorithms and refining data analysis techniques.

Her work focused on improving the sensitivity of radio telescopes to detect faint, potentially artificial signals from distant star systems.

Peggy's contributions were crucial in enhancing the program's ability to sift through cosmic noise and focus on promising signals, making her an integral part of the SETI team.

Tim and Peggy's colleagues admired the couple's dedication to deep space exploration and finding the first Goldilocks planet with advanced life.

Many of their new work friends were invited to Tim and Peggy's house for electric grill barbecues, held indoors during the 95-degree-plus afternoons.

Dr. Maya Patel, a brilliant astrophysicist specializing in planetary atmospheres, was also on the SETI team. She brought expertise in analyzing and understanding the atmospheric conditions of distant planets to the Goldilocks team.

Her work focused on determining whether the atmospheres of these planets could support life by studying their composition, weather patterns, and potential for sustaining water in liquid form. Maya's deep understanding of atmospheric science enabled the team to identify critical indicators of habitability, such as the presence of oxygen, nitrogen, and other life-sustaining gases.

Maya's innovative research techniques, including advanced spectroscopy and climate modeling, allowed the team to accurately assess the conditions on these far-off worlds.

Another colleague, Major Mark Andrews, a cheerful former Navy pilot and astronaut turned space scientist, brought lighthearted energy to the team and invaluable expertise in spacecraft navigation, communication and planetary exploration.

He was also best friends with Leonard Bouchard and piloted one of the Mars missions they both crewed. Mark's experience and dependability made him an essential asset in the team's quest to discover habitable planets.

Mark and Leonard's leadership skills, honed through military and space missions, made them vital contributors to the team's collaborative efforts.

Tim's contribution to the project was pivotal, not just because of his deep understanding of astrophysics and innovative problem-solving approach, but also because he had the one intangible that made him a key player in the search for these distant worlds—ESP.

The Milky Way is massive, with 100 billion to 400 billion stars and 100,000 light-years across, and it is just a medium-sized galaxy. Narrowing down where to look for exoplanets in the Milky Way took as much luck as science.

Tim's psychic abilities gave him an edge on where to look. And he had a pretty good idea.

CHAPTER 5:
DISCOVERY OF TERRA NOVA

Kennedy Space Center, September 4, 2077

Tim Smith leaned over the control panel, his fingers flying across the touch-sensitive surface as he adjusted the parameters of the holographic display. The room around him was bathed in the soft glow of screens and floating data streams, each a testament to the monumental task that had consumed the Goldilocks team for decades.

More than 100 years after Astronaut Neil Armstrong became the first human to walk on the Moon, NASA's technological prowess reached unprecedented heights, allowing humanity to travel further and peer deeper into the cosmos.

The Goldilocks project had grown from its humble beginnings with the Hubble Space Telescope, enhanced by the James Webb Space Telescope, to a vast network of ultra-high-resolution telescopes stationed far beyond the moon's orbit.

These telescopes, enhanced with advanced gravitational

lenses that acted like natural magnifying glasses, enabled the SETI team to detect and analyze exoplanets in extraordinary detail.

But it wasn't just the telescopes that made the difference. Over the years, NASA developed quantum-based technologies that revolutionized the field of astrophysics. These technologies allowed for real-time data processing and analysis, enabling scientists to study the atmospheres of distant exoplanets as if they were just next door.

By the time Tim joined NASA, the Goldilocks project had moved beyond merely identifying exoplanets; it could now analyze the chemical composition of their atmospheres and even detect biosignatures—specific molecules or patterns that suggested the presence of life.

Tim's heart raced as data came streaming in. He had been monitoring a planet 12 light-years away in the constellation Cetus (the whale), a region known for its abundance of orange and red dwarf stars. This particular star, an orange dwarf, had captured Tim's attention due to the unusual magnetic signals emanating from one of its orbiting planets.

Tim had a special feeling about the star system for several days.

As Tim refined the data, the image of the planet came into sharper focus. It was breathtakingly similar to Earth—a sizeable rocky world with vast oceans, swirling clouds, and a surface dotted with green continents.

The atmospheric analysis confirmed it: this planet, for which Tim had already chosen a name—Terra Nova—had an atmosphere rich in oxygen and nitrogen, with traces of water vapor, strong indicators of the potential for life.

It was a world where life could thrive, a "second Earth" nestled within the orange dwarf's habitable zone. But there was more. As the data continued to pour in, Tim felt a familiar sensation—a tingling at the base of his skull, a sign that his psychic abilities were stirring.

These abilities, awakened years ago by his exposure to the mysterious space rock containing the unique and strange element newvidium, which Dr. Ledbetter had named, had often guided him in his work. They told him that Terra Nova was more than a habitable world. There was something else, something alive, calling out across the void.

With a deep breath, Tim closed his eyes and focused. Images and sensations flooded his mind—visions of alien landscapes teeming with life and a sense of something … intelligent.

He didn't have the data, but he knew, with absolute certainty, that Terra Nova wasn't just a mirror of Earth; it was home to something extraordinary.

Tim's eyes snapped open. It was time to call in Peggy, Leonard, and the rest of the Goldilocks team.

"Peggy, come over. I've found it—Terra Nova," Tim whispered into his wristphone, trying to contain his enthusiasm.

Five minutes later, Peggy, Leonard, Dr. Maya Patel and Major Mark Andrews gathered around the holographic display. Their faces ranged from awe to disbelief as Tim showed them the evidence: the spectral lines indicating oxygen and water vapor, the faint but distinct biosignatures in the planet's atmosphere, and the possibility—no, the probability—of intelligent life.

"Terra Nova? That's what you are going to call it?" Peggy said excitedly, her eyes wide as she stared at the image of the new Earth. "This changes everything."

Leonard, the seasoned engineer and space veteran, touched Tim's shoulder. "You've done it, Tim. You've found the new world we've been searching for so long to find."

Tim nodded, his mind racing with the implications. "Terra Nova," he said softly, the name felt right on his tongue.

"What do you think, Maya?" Tim asked.

"Terra Nova? I like it. The data looks very similar to Earth, minus our man-made pollution. I am reading fluctuating methane and oxygen levels, suggesting plant and animal life, which is an excellent sign. I want to run some models to confirm your initial findings," she said.

"I'll let NASA's command center know what we found," said Leonard.

"We better order some strong coffee. I have a feeling nobody is going anywhere tonight," Mark said as he surveyed the team, which was already focused on the job ahead.

As the team worked tirelessly through the night, the holographic image of Terra Nova continued to rotate slowly in the center of the room, a constant reminder of what they had found.

Within a week, Terra Nova became the focus of intense study from astronomers worldwide.

China announced it would send a nuclear fusion-powered probe toward Terra Nova. Packed with long-range detectors, the Chinese believed the probe could gather more data once it left the Solar System.

Russia and India, which had advanced lunar bases equipped with long-range telescopes, redirected their focus toward Terra Nova, demonstrating their commitment to understanding and potentially engaging with the newly discovered planet.

Indian astrophysicists began collaborating closely with their Russian counterparts, combining their technological strengths and expertise in a joint mission to probe deeper into the mysteries of Terra Nova.

Space scientists enhanced their telescopic arrays to maximize their observational capabilities. They hoped to gather detailed data on Terra Nova's atmospheric composition, potential signs of life, and any technological signals that might emanate from the planet.

Once the Internet, newspapers, radio, bloggers and others reported the findings, a global debate began about the implications of finding life beyond Earth.

Churches claimed that God created other worlds based on Earth. Scientists explained the news as expected, considering there are more than two trillion galaxies and counting in the known universe.

After President Carlin announced the news, the global scientific community wondered whether this could lead to the first contact with an extraterrestrial civilization and, if so, what intentions the extraterrestrial lifeforms might have.

The United Nations convened to discuss the highly

sensitive and critical proposals about sending a short-burst photon message to Terra Nova.

The debate highlighted the profound implications of attempting contact with an unknown civilization potentially residing in a distant galaxy.

Proponents argued that the photon message, encoded with humanity's peaceful intentions, could be a first step in establishing communication, potentially opening the door to interstellar diplomacy or knowledge exchange.

On the other hand, skeptics within the assembly raised concerns about the risks involved, particularly the uncertainty of Terra Nova's technological and cultural development.

Given humanity's limitations in understanding the receiving civilization, they questioned whether such a message might be perceived as a threat and trigger unintended consequences.

NASA took another approach. Based on Tim's suggestions, Terra Nova would be studied, and more data would be collected before any communication was attempted.

Besides, at 12 light years away, Terra Nova was too distant to make it worthwhile to send advanced probes or deploy reconnaissance satellites, even with light sails propelled by powerful lasers and fusion drives. Any direct contact would take more than 50 years to produce results.

Tim warned NASA that Terra Nova could present a danger. He was asked for data to support his danger theory. All he had was a sense of unease, a deep-rooted intuition that this planet could pose a significant threat to Earth. He couldn't prove why.

But as Tim's frustration grew with his lack of data, the first tremors of an inexplicable cosmic event began to ripple through the solar system, proving his fears might be more than a hunch.

CHAPTER 6:
DYING EARTH

Sarasota and the World, 2067-2069

By the mid-21st century, climate change and global warming had become an inescapable reality for humanity.

Between 1900 and 2069, atmospheric carbon dioxide levels doubled to 550 parts per million, accelerating the melting of glaciers and icebergs. This, in turn, caused global sea levels to rise by two feet, leading to widespread tidal flooding in the United States and other coastal regions.

The warming planet also spurred the spread of tropical and insect-borne diseases such as Lyme disease and West Nile Virus, and frequent pandemics across the globe that caused respiratory, heart and brain-related diseases.

Consequently, casual international travel nearly stopped as nations struggled to contain outbreaks and protect their populations.

Natural disasters like hurricanes, typhoons, floods, heat waves, and wildfires continued to strike the Earth with increasing intensity, injuries and deaths.

Despite the chaos, Tim's parents wanted to expose him

to the outdoors and teach him skills they hoped would help him survive in the worsening environment.

From age six through nine, Tim spent summers in the mountains of North Carolina, where camp counselors taught him outdoor survival skills, such as camping, hiking, swimming, fishing, archery and shooting. They also taught him self-reliance, teamwork and leadership. On camping trips, Tim also learned about the night sky, planets, and stars.

Little did his parents know that Tim would be exposed to the strange powers of the space rock, granting him powers and abilities that far exceeded what he learned at Camp Waybegone.

But growing up during the massive climate change of the 2060s, Tim was profoundly impacted by the stark realities of a world in upheaval. Every year, it seemed, extreme weather events became worse. Rising sea levels and environmental degradation became the unsettling norm, shaping his deep concern for the planet's future.

Where he lived, on Florida's Gulf Coast, cities like Sarasota were grappling with climate challenges. The warming Atlantic Ocean and the Gulf of Mexico gave the conditions that led to more intense and destructive storms and hurricanes.

The Florida coastline was also experiencing rising sea levels, which, combined with more intense storms, put communities such as Sarasota and dozens of others at risk.

Saltwater intrusion into freshwater supplies and the loss of critical habitats like mangroves and wetlands further underscored the region's vulnerability.

All of Florida was vulnerable to how greenhouse gases

in the atmosphere were changing the Earth. Rising sea levels on the state's East Coast led to frequent flooding and shoreline erosion.

The Atlantic Ocean's relentless advance had made areas like Cape Canaveral on Merritt Island increasingly vulnerable, prompting NASA to move its operations inland to safeguard its missions and infrastructure.

Down further south, low-lying areas like Miami and the Florida Keys faced significant sea-level rise, frequent coastal flooding, and dreadful impacts from stronger hurricanes.

Rising air temperatures led to more intense heat waves, straining energy systems and increasing health risks. As living costs and threats increased, a steady stream of people relocated to safer inland areas or northern states.

Florida's long coasts and flat geography made it particularly susceptible to the consequences of a warming planet.

Tim, sensitive to the changes around him and hearing the stories from real people affected, dreamed of a better future.

When he was 13, Tim had his first memorable vision of a dying Earth.

Tim found himself standing on a desolate, cracked landscape. The air was thick with heat, each breath a struggle.

In the distance, the horizon shimmered with the unnatural glow of intense wildfires, casting an eerie red hue across the sky. The ground beneath his feet trembled as another earthquake rippled through the Earth, splitting the terrain and causing ancient trees to topple.

Suddenly, he was transported to a coastal city. The streets were rivers submerged under the relentless rise of the sea. Skyscrapers jutted out of the water like gravestones, their lower levels consumed by the ocean.

People scrambled to higher ground, their faces etched with despair and panic. He heard the distant rumble of a volcano erupting, spewing ash and molten lava, the sky darkening as if the world were closing its eyes.

In another flash, Tim saw vast deserts where lush forests once thrived. The ground was parched and lifeless, the vegetation reduced to brittle twigs and sand.

Communities fought over dwindling water supplies, conflicts erupting into violent skirmishes. Those local disputes broke into regional wars as nations battled for dwindling resources such as clean water and arable land.

Tim woke to see the desperate and displaced faces merging into a faceless mass of humanity struggling to survive.

Like most dreams, Tim recalled every detail. Because they were recurring, he believed it was a sign of his future calling.

Over the next two years, young Tim was determined to dedicate his life to fighting climate change. He told his supportive parents he planned to study environmental, atmospheric and climatology science in college. He would help find solutions to global warming and help save Earth from its looming crisis. They supported him, especially his mother.

But as he grew older, turning 15, Tim started having visions of deep space, the vast, mysterious expanse filled with billions of stars, nebulae, black holes, and dark matter. He hadn't any specific visions of life on other planets. Still, he became increasingly drawn to space sciences, particularly astrophysics, as a field he wanted to know more about.

Shortly after his 17th birthday, when his high school counselor asked him what he wanted to study in college, he blurted out he wanted to be an astrophysicist.

While the Earth's decline was an urgent and undeniable reality, pulling many of his peers, including his best friend George Clarke, into climate change fields, Tim felt an inexplicable pull toward the mysteries of the cosmos. Something important was out there. He sensed a future vision would reveal itself one day.

Besides, despite his recurring visions of a dying Earth, he felt the solutions to its problems lay beyond its atmosphere, hidden in the vastness of deep space. He sensed that astrophysics, understanding the universe, could offer insights or technologies that might ultimately help save Earth.

More importantly, he wondered, was life out there in deep space waiting to be discovered? He sensed it. However, he hadn't any visions to prove it. But if so, and he increasingly believed it accurate, there must be an advanced civilization somewhere in the universe that could help Earth.

CHAPTER 7:
THE WORMHOLE VISION

Titusville, Nov. 15, 2077

Tim was floating in space, surrounded by the silent void. Stars twinkled in the distance, but there was an unsettling stillness. Suddenly, a faint sound began to pierce the silence, growing louder and more precise.

A strange alien voice echoed through his mind: "*We are coming. We are coming.*"

He awoke. *We are coming?* He had heard these words at Camp Waybegone right after exposure to the space rock, the dust and the purple gas. Why had he forgotten it until now?

Peggy was beside him, sleeping. He didn't want to wake her. He closed his eyes again, concentrated, and saw himself floating in space. He heard the voice again. "*We are coming. We are coming.*"

Silently, he asked, "Who is it?"

A shape formed. Initially hazy and out of focus, it became more apparent. He saw it, an enormous spacecraft, its surface bristling with unfamiliar technology, moving with deliberate menace toward Earth.

The voice repeated, "*We are coming. We are coming.*"

Still floating in space, he felt the void around him close in, the vast emptiness enveloping him. The voice grew louder, more insistent, and the spaceship loomed ever closer.

Again, he silently asked, "Who are you?"

Tim's heart pounded. He gasped because he saw them. Aliens, breathing air like Earthlings, were on the spaceship. They were tall, pale, and spindly, with big eyes and heads, small ears and mouths.

Again, he silently asked, "Where are you from?"

The voice replied, "*We come from Terra Nova.*"

Excited, he silently asked, "How did you get here?"

"*Witness,*" the voice said.

Tim saw a giant spacecraft entering a bright-edged, tunnel-like path, a wormhole near Terra Nova. It traveled magically through the wormhole, surrounded by glittering stars, gaseous nebulas and spinning galaxies. After a dizzying time, the spacecraft exited the wormhole, which he sensed was located in the Solar System past Neptune and in the Kuiper belt's inner reaches.

The voice repeated, "*We are coming. We are coming.*"

As the vision abruptly ended, Tim leaped out of bed onto his feet. With the voice echoing in his mind, he landed on the floor with a thud.

The noise jolted Peggy awake. She turned and exclaimed in a sleepy, concerned voice, "What is it? What happened?"

Gasping, Tim stood beside the bed. Wide-eyed, he tried to understand the imminent event and possible danger he had just witnessed.

"Tim, talk to me," Peggy said as she got up and rushed to him.

He stood there, shivering. It is true, he thought. Aliens on a spaceship. They are coming from Terra Nova.

"You're cold. Tim, tell me what you saw," she said.

"It is happening. Peg, I've got to tell you everything," he said as he sat on the bed.

"Wait, I am still getting bits and pieces from this vision. It's jumbled, but I'm getting a clearer picture."

"Are you all right? Talk with me," Peggy insisted.

He sat there with his eyes open. He saw aliens on a planet, in a spaceship, in protective, environmentally controlled sleep chambers. Then he heard a voice calling, *"Help us! Help us!"*

Tim went limp and slumped over. Peggy held him and pushed him back onto the bed. She positioned his head on the pillow and stretched him out on the bed. He was breathing deeply. She knew he had experienced a vivid dream and needed a few minutes to recover.

As he slept, Peggy went to the bathroom. She washed her hands and splashed water on her face. Looking in the mirror, she wondered what Tim had seen.

Two minutes later, she heard Tim stirring and walked into the bedroom.

"Tim, are you all right?"

"Yes," he said, flustered and nervous. "I don't feel well."

"You need a few minutes to recover. Maybe you should lie down. It's still early, not even 5 a.m."

"No, I need to take a cold shower and get dressed," Tim said.

"Can you stand up?"

"Yes," said Tim as he slowly rose from the bed. "Please, can you make coffee? I'll be better after I shower and have a shot of Joe. You know how it is."

"All right, but you scared me," she said.

After a few seconds, Tim's head cleared.

"Wow, that was a strong reaction, but it's over. I'll feel much better after my shower." He kissed her and said, "I've got a story for you. Just wait a few minutes." Then he walked into the bathroom.

She followed him in to make sure he was better. "I'm worried. You collapsed."

"It's okay. I'll be a few minutes in the bathroom," he said.

"All right. I'll make some coffee," she said.

As he turned on the water, Tim wondered if Peggy, her father, George, Maya, Mark and the others would believe an alien spacecraft was headed toward Earth from a planet 12 light years away.

Tim knew it was time he told Peggy everything. She needed to know. His vision was a dire warning, a glimpse into a rapidly approaching future.

Peggy sipped her coffee as he entered the kitchen. He was fully dressed and ready for work. She was still wearing short pajama pants and a T-shirt.

She stood up and went to him.

"Tim, you seem better? Sit down and have a coffee. Tell me, what's the matter? Did you have a bad dream? You tossed and turned most of the night and then jumped out of bed. What is it?" she asked.

"It was awful," he said.

"What was? You said you would tell me everything."

"Yes, it's time you know the whole story," he said as he walked over to the coffee pot and poured himself a cup.

Peggy froze. She knew what that meant. Whatever awful thing Tim experienced during the night, telling her his secret meant it was big.

He turned to her, looked at her baby blue eyes and said, "It started at Camp Waybegone. I was nine."

Peggy stood there with her mouth open. She had been waiting for this explanation almost since she had met him. Like her father, she sensed something otherworldly about him. He had always refused to explain or talk about it.

Tim spent five minutes explaining what happened at Camp Waybegone. He told her how he found the shiny space rock, how he picked it up, how it crumbled, and how it released the purple gas and dust.

"I started seeing the future, glimpses of what would happen, what people would say and do," said Tim.

"I suspected something happened at summer camp," she said. "I always thought you were super smart and had the most unique color of eyes, but there was something else. A space rock?"

"When I was exposed to the space rock's dust and gas, my eyes changed from light blue to purplish blue," Tim said. "Dr. Ledbetter has never been able to discover how that is connected to my psychic powers, but it is the only physical change."

"I should have known. What else?" she asked.

"Well, after I was exposed, I pretended not to remember anything," Tim said. "Only George Clarke, Stephen Martin, Dr. Charles Ledbetter, Nurse Paula Winters, and my parents know anything about that day."

"They all know this story, and I don't?" Peggy exclaimed.

"They were there at the time," Tim said. "I got them to promise not to say anything, ever. But even they don't know what I will tell you now."

"Go on," she said.

"As I said, when I woke up at the camp infirmary, I couldn't remember what happened when I picked up the space rock. Then, a few minutes later, I remembered the whole thing," he said.

"You lied to them? Why?" she asked.

"People asked what happened when I picked up the space rock and collapsed. All I know is I was drawn to it, and the next thing I knew, I was in the infirmary with Nurse Paula asking questions. I started seeing the future, which was scary and overwhelming. Not wanting to explain something I didn't understand, I pretended nothing happened," Tim said.

"All this happened when you were only nine?" Peggy asked.

"Yes. I learned to block the visions. It took me years to fully control my foresight and visions of the future," Tim said. "Remember when we met in history class? I saw you and thought of you and had a vision about us in the future. We were together and married."

"You saw us married the moment you saw me?" Peggy blurted out. "You acted so normal when we first met. Very nice and helpful. This explains a lot."

"Some visions are like snapshots. I knew we were right for each other," Tim said, pausing. "I love you, my darling."

"Oh, Tim, I love you, but why didn't you tell me this

sooner?"

Tim held her hand. "I didn't want to scare you," he said softly. "We just met. We seemed so natural together. Maybe you felt it something as well?"

"I didn't initially, but you were nice, funny, and calm. I thought it was meant to be," Peggy said.

"It was. I decided to wait to tell you this story until you were ready. Now, you need to know what is coming."

Stunned, Peggy looked at Tim.

"What is coming? What do you mean?"

Tim looked at her and wondered if she would understand.

"You had one of these visions last night?" Peggy asked. "What is it? It must have been something serious to make you want to tell me now."

"Yes," he said. "It was a vision of the future."

"What is it?" she asked. "Did you see something in space? On Earth? Something about us?"

"You are nearly right," Tim said. "I saw a vision of something in space coming to Earth. I have to tell you so you can help me get ready."

"What is coming from space?" she firmly asked.

Tim paused, deciding how to tell her.

"This is going to be hard. You should sit down," Tim said.

"What did you see?" she asked.

"An alien spaceship," he finally said, waiting for a response from her.

She was speechless for a few seconds, then smiled. "Tim, let's take the day off. You need to tell me a lot more than you had a vision of an alien spaceship."

"I will, but we need to go to the grocery store," Tim said.

"What? Why? What do you want?" she asked.

"Maybe a doughnut," he said with a straight face.

"You are joking. You don't eat doughnuts."

"Trust me on this. First, the grocery store., and I promise you will know everything as soon as I do. Just humor me for now. Let's go," Tim said.

"I need to take a shower and dress for work. Can the grocery store wait for that?" she asked with a smile.

"Go ahead," he said, pouring another cup of coffee. "I'll be outside. I want to see the sunrise."

Tim walked outside. The sun was peeking over the horizon, and he knew what to do.

Peggy rushed into the bedroom and ripped off her summer pajamas. She wondered what else Tim would tell her about his past and the vision. Ten minutes later, Peggy was dressed and ready to go. She knew how quickly to act when Tim was this way.

She came out a few minutes later. Tim was gazing toward the east. The sun had just risen.

"Where are we going?" she asked as she opened the door of her electric Ford Focus.

"Publix," he said.

"What is on your mind? What else did you see?"

"Something is going to happen soon out in the cosmos. We will soon experience theoretical physics in real-time," Tim mysteriously said.

"Really? C'mon, tell me the whole story," Peggy demanded as she backed up the car.

"All right," he said. "You aren't going to like it."

As she drove, Tim told her about the wormhole he saw opening past Neptune and the alien spaceship's fusion drive igniting.

"You heard them say, 'We are coming, we are coming?'" Peggy said.

"I heard them, and I know what they look like," Tim said.

CHAPTER 8:
POWERBALL

Morning, Nov. 15, 2077

Peggy drove to the grocery store and pulled into the parking lot. Tim got out and walked in. He knew exactly where he was going. The sign at the customer service counter read "Powerball Jackpot: $100 Million."

Six numbers flashed vividly in his mind, almost as if they were being projected directly into his thoughts. 8-14-27-32-54-58.

Tim purchased a Powerball, carefully selecting the numbers that had appeared in his mind. He sensed something extraordinary was about to happen.

He put the ticket in his pocket and walked outside to the car.

"What did you get?" Peggy asked as he opened the door and sat down.

"A winning Powerball ticket," he said.

"You had a vision about winning a lottery ticket?" she asked. "What's the jackpot?"

"One hundred million. We are going to need the money," he said. "This is just the start of what we need to do. Let's go to work. We need to talk with your father."

"My father? Is he part of your vision about the alien spaceship?" she asked.

"In a way. There is a lot more I need to tell you, just not in this parking lot," Tim said.

"I need to know everything," Peggy said as she steered the car onto the highway toward Kennedy.

"I promised. You and your father will be told the whole plan together," Tim said.

As Peggy drove to Kennedy, she thought about how much she loved Tim. She knew all along he was exceptional, and he had a secret. But had no idea it was something like this. She was learning so much about him. She also had so much to think about. A space rock that gave Tim psychic powers? A vision about a wormhole opening in the Kuiper belt? An alien ship on its way to Earth? He knows what the aliens look like? And then, he will win a $100 million Powerball jackpot? To use for what?

After a few minutes of silence, she asked, "I am glad you want to tell my father about all this, but does he need to know for a particular reason?"

"Yes, of course. I need permission to use the James Webb Space Telescope."

"The Space Telescope? Why?"

"They are coming, and I need to find them."

"They? Are you talking about the alien spaceship that will emerge soon from a wormhole in the Kuiper belt? I can't wait to see my father's reaction when you tell him that," Peggy said with a smile.

"I wonder if he will be surprised when I tell him they are coming from Terra Nova," Tim said.

"Terra Nova? The Earth-like planet you discovered?"

Peggy exclaimed. "The aliens are coming from Terra Nova?"

"Yes, keep driving. I want to get to work. Your father needs to know, and there's little time to waste," Tim said.

As Peggy drove, she wondered what else she would discover about her husband. He was the same person, yet his revelation about psychic powers, a wormhole and a spaceship filled with aliens from Terra Nova scared her because it meant their lives would change in ways she couldn't fathom.

"You will tell me when you have your next vision, won't you?" she asked.

"Of course," he said. "You're my wife."

Tim had a pretty good idea of what would happen next. He didn't need another vision.

He was confident he would win the $100 million Powerball jackpot that night. After paying 30% in income taxes, he would receive $70 million.

He had a specific plan for the money. Since the vision earlier that morning, everything seemed surreal. It wasn't just because of the massive fortune he knew he would win. It was because the vision confirmed everything he knew about the dying Earth and the danger from space.

He was also certain that billions would die before the aliens were stopped. Tim knew they would be stopped. How, he wasn't sure yet.

CHAPTER 9

BUILDING A SAFE HAVEN

Sarasota, December 2077 – April 2078

With his newfound wealth, Tim bought 25 acres in east Sarasota County, near his hometown. Because of the county's high elevation, he thought it would be safer than near the Kennedy Space Center in Titusville.

On weekends, Tim and Peggy drove to Sarasota and met with an architect, a contractor and a builder. Soon, they had a design for a two-story house, a garage, an underground shelter, and a renewable energy system.

The self-sustaining bioshelter was located on a property 30 feet above sea level, nearly the highest elevation in Sarasota County. It was surrounded by rolling fields and dense woodlands, which offered a sense of seclusion and security.

Construction began on the project in mid-December.

Tim's bioshelter called for a 5,000-square-foot, energy-efficient home atop a 10,000-square-foot, state-of-the-art underground fallout shelter. It was designed for 50 people and could be expanded to accommodate 100.

The purchase of the land and the construction of the

house and underground shelter were necessary preparations for the impending events.

This was just the start.

<hr>

One bright Saturday morning in mid-April, Tim and Peggy drove southwest three hours to Sarasota from their home in Titusville. Six months after Tim won the Powerball jackpot, the couple was anxious to review their house and underground bioshelter.

"Do you think the work will be completed this time?" said Peggy. "They promised last month it would be done."

"We've had some supply and installation problems, especially with the biogas digester, the water filtration system and the computer upgrades to link to NASA's deep space probes and the JWST," Tim said.

"Yes, but Maya and Mark have been working with your contractors, and your brother, Tom and Nick have been making sure the construction designs and specs have been carried out according to plan," Peggy said. "Do you think that will be enough?"

"On the NASA link, yes. The last time Mark was there, he said he made the necessary changes to get the link working on our end. He said he would make the adjustments at the Kennedy end, and all we need to do is turn it on and run diagnostics," Tim said.

"He should know," Peggy said.

"Regarding the other systems, we can fix them if they aren't working. Nick will come out and take care of it. He is a maintenance wizard. I don't foresee any problems with our bioshelter we can't handle."

"Then what's been on your mind this trip? You've been unusually quiet. What is it?" Peggy asked.

"Oh, the usual. The degrading biosphere of our planet, the alien spaceship headed to Earth, and why I can't get a sense of what is happening inside it," said Tim with a tinge of sarcasm. "Other than that."

"I am sure everything will be revealed when it's time," said Peggy reassuringly.

But Tim felt a sense of urgency as they neared the property—time was running out. He didn't want to worry Peggy unduly. Enough was happening with the world on high alert, and their plans to move to the house and bioshelter were well underway.

Any day now, he sensed that the aliens would travel through the wormhole as his vision had predicted. Very soon, he would have to spend extra time looking for the spaceship through the James Webb Space Telescope. He dreaded how the world would react to the news.

Up ahead, Peggy saw the turn to the house and bioshelter. It was a mile off the main highway.

"Finally, we are here," said Peggy with a smile. "You know we've been coming here practically every weekend for the past month, and I still get excited. But I have to ask, why does it seem to take longer when you drive?"

Tim laughed. "You like this joke. I know you like it a lot better when Mark flies us in his jet.

"I know. I got spoiled. It's so fast, and he lands in the grass field 500 yards from our house," Peggy said. "We are 30 minutes away from Titusville by jet!"

"Mark is busy at NASA this weekend working on our

link. Besides, we have the equipment and other things in the SUV we needed to bring this weekend," Tim said.

"I hope we have some help to unload," Peggy said.

"We will. Everyone should get here later this afternoon," Tim said.

"Are your parents going to be here today?" Peggy asked.

"They promised. Dad wants to come, but Mom is hesitant. She has known that these visions mean terrible things will happen, and she is afraid," Tim said.

"I need to talk with her," said Peggy.

"She'd like that," Tim said. "We haven't had much time with everything going on."

Tim slowed his Ford Explorer Hybrid SUV to get ready to turn into the dirt road leading to their property's gate and U-shaped driveway. He turned in and drove a few hundred feet until approaching an eight-foot steel fence surrounding the entrance. He pulled up, stopped, rolled his window down and leaned his head out enough for the security screen to scan his face.

"Tim Smith. RS2484T," he said, and the electronically operated gate opened.

All visitors, including Tim, entering the property encountered the facial recognition and password security system. Two hidden micro-video cameras also monitored the entrance. The security system was connected to a computer that only allowed certain people to enter. Others needed human approval.

The entire property was surrounded by a barbed wire perimeter fence behind a three-foot-deep drainage ditch to prevent vehicles from entering.

Driving up to the house, Tim noticed no worker trucks

in the yard and all the garage doors were closed.

Nestled amidst the lush Florida landscape, the two-story house's sleek, modern lines stood out against the backdrop of palms and native vegetation. Its exterior was a fusion of stone and glass that shimmered in the late morning light.

"Just as promised, they finished the house," Tim said.

"Oh, it looks magnificent," Peggy exclaimed.

Flanking the left and right sides of the property and rising from the backyard, three sleek windmills turned steadily in the breeze. Their blades captured the wind's energy with a soft whoosh to generate power around the clock.

Solar panels glinted on the slanted roof, angled to capture every bit of sunlight throughout the day to supply additional electricity.

Beneath the house, hidden from view, were large underground tanks filled with gasoline and diesel, stored as a backup power source for the heavy-duty generators. This system ensured that the shelter and home could remain self-sufficient for many months.

"George did a great job designing our renewable energy system," Peggy said.

"He is one of the top environmental engineers in Florida, maybe the U.S.," Tim said.

"And your best friend," Peggy said. "It was nice that George transferred to UF during his senior year so I could spend time with him. Now that you've told me the space rock story and I know how he and Stephen Martin were also affected by the gas and dust newvidium, he and I have become closer."

"He was almost as happy as you when he learned I told you the Camp Waybegone story," Tim said with a chuckle. "Of course, I got the full exposure to the space rock, but his smaller exposure still gave him enough psychic powers and insight to help him develop advanced environmental programs. He can talk with you about it now."

"I wonder when I will meet Stephen Martin," Peggy said. "It's strange you haven't introduced me to him and his wife Julie."

"Hopefully, you will meet him soon. Honestly, he became reclusive a few years ago. I'll explain another time. I hope I can work it out with him. I need him to help us with the alien threat," Tim said.

"Does he have the same powers as you?" Peggy asked.

"No, but much more than George," Tim said. "After his exposure, he started to change, personality-wise. George is pretty much the same. But Stephen's wife is also very private. You'll like her, although she is a bit shy. I talk regularly with Stephen over the phone, but that's been it for the past few years."

"Sometimes I wish we lived a normal life," Peggy said. "I know we are lucky to be alive, given everything happening in the world."

"Yes, but look at what we have. It's our safe place. Don't you feel safe here?" Tim said.

"I feel safe whenever I am with you," Peggy sighed.

Tim nodded. He remembered when he was nine and how things were simpler at Camp Waybegone before his exposure.

But that was then, and this was now.

Looking out over the land, the house, the hidden

underground bioshelter and everything else, Tim felt a deep satisfaction—this was more than just a piece of land and buildings; it was a sanctuary.

As Tim and Peggy approached their refuge, they felt a palpable sense of unease. Despite the scenic surroundings, it hung in the air. The world outside was growing increasingly uncertain, with the looming threat of the alien spaceship, escalating tensions in the Middle East, and the worsening impacts of climate change.

The house itself exuded a quiet, unassuming luxury. A wide driveway, lined with meticulously trimmed greenery, led up to the six-car garage, its doors seamless with the structure.

The main entrance to the underground bioshelter was inside the oversized garage. Beyond the house, tucked discreetly into the rear of the property under trees, was an emergency entrance/exit to the bioshelter. Its only visible sign was a reinforced steel hatch flanked by ventilation shafts.

Tim parked the SUV near the front, and as they stepped out, both felt a mix of pride and apprehension.

"Jeff and Tom said they'd be out later to show us what they've done the past week," Tim said.

"What time did he say he'd be out with Amy?" Peggy asked.

"About 2 p.m. Jeff said he would bring some freshly caught fish for grilling. Tom will be out later with Mary. Did I tell you that Steve and Sophie might also come out?" Tim said.

"We should have quite a weekend. It's still hard for me to wrap my head around why we built this beautiful house and shelter," Peggy said. "It is a dream vacation home, except what we are doing isn't a dream."

"We are in survival mode," said Tim as he led Peggy to the front door and opened it with an electronic key. "Well, here we are. Let's take a look."

CHAPTER 10:
THE UNDERGROUND BIOSHELTER

NASA Station Sarasota, April 2078

Tim and Peggy's two-story house, perched above the underground shelter, was a model of sustainable energy.

As they entered, they were greeted by an airy, open foyer bathed in natural light. The smooth, polished stone floors extended into the living space, giving the interior a sleek yet warm feel.

Just to the left of the front door, a high-tech control panel glowed softly on the wall, displaying critical information: battery power supplied by the windmills and solar panels, the house's internal temperature and the air filtration levels. Data on the underground bioshelter was protected by a passcode only Tim and Peggy knew.

Tim glanced at the control panel, reassured by the steady flow of electricity and perfect climate control.

Walking into the spacious living room, visible from the foyer, was minimalist yet comfortable. Plush, modern furniture in neutral tones contrasted against the warm oak beams overhead. A sizeable wall-mounted video screen displayed an image of deep space.

"Is this Steve's idea of a joke?" Peggy asked.

"In a way, yes," Tim replied. "He also probably wanted to show us the link to NASA's space probes work. He's been working closely with Mark on it for weeks."

They noticed smart lighting that adjusted its brightness automatically as they walked through the living room. Floor-to-ceiling windows framed a view of the wind turbines and the dozen orange, grapefruit and tangerine trees on the side and backyards.

As they moved toward the kitchen, the house revealed its high-tech nature. Every detail had been crafted for both luxury and sustainability. Touch-sensitive glass doors slid open to a sleek dining area with a reclaimed wood table that offered seating for family and guests.

Beyond that, the gourmet kitchen featured gleaming stainless-steel appliances, granite countertops, and an island with a built-in induction stove. On one wall, a control panel with LED displays showed updates on weather, energy consumption, and the bioshelter's hydroponic garden's growth status.

"I still can't get over how well you designed this kitchen. Unless the aliens change their minds, we may only use it for a month before we go underground," Peggy said.

"They won't. Chef Nancy is responsible for the house kitchen and the bioshelter kitchen. I told her I wanted to spare no expense and that creating a gourmet house kitchen would help disguise our underground bioshelter to protect against intruders," Tim said.

"When are Nancy and Carlos coming to set up our

bioshelter kitchen and food service?" Peggy asked.

"Hard to say. Whenever I confirm the alien spaceship entering our Solar System," Tim said. "Everybody is on standby until that happens."

"You feel it is soon?" Peggy said.

"Yes, very soon," Tim said.

Tim pointed out to Peggy the large touchscreen monitor near the pantry, where, using his passcode, he could access the food inventory of the underground bioshelter. He could also input another code to open a hidden doorway leading to a concealed staircase to access the underground supply room.

"I wonder if we have food," said Peggy as she opened the fridge, which was stocked based on their orders. It was all there. Fresh milk, orange juice, eggs, meat, bread, fruits and vegetables were on the shelves.

The rest of the downstairs included a dining room, a den and computer room, an entertainment room and two bathrooms, one with a shower.

Upstairs were five bedrooms, each with a full bathroom and another entertainment room. The third level, the roof, where the solar panels lay, included an observatory platform with a telescope mount for old-fashioned night sky viewing.

After inspecting their house, Tim suggested they bring the suitcases and equipment from the SUV and trailer into the garage. Fifteen minutes later, they were done.

"Could we take a quick walk through the bioshelter?" Peggy said. "I'm curious how it looks."

"Do you mind if we do that later when everyone arrives?" Tim said. "I'm hungry. We ate breakfast hours ago. What's for lunch?"

"I can make sandwiches if you help," Peggy said

After eating, they sat on the sofa in the living room and watched the worldwide news. A little after 2 p.m., a purple security light flashed on Tim's wristphone, and a beeping sound came from the house's speaker system.

"Arriving at the front gate is Jeff and Amy Smith. I also scan Steve and Sophie Flatt and Dr. Bill and Martha Flatt with them. Should I open the gate?" said Al, the computer artificial intelligence voice from the house computer.

"Yes, Al, let them in," Tim said.

"Should we call Tom to see when he will arrive?" Peggy asked.

"Call Mary," Tim said. "I am sure they will be later."

During the week, Jeff, Steve, Nick and Tom spent as much time as they could helping to oversee the construction. Tim had hired Tom's contractor father, Paul Terry, to build the house and shelter, but Tim liked having feedback from his brother and three friends.

Tim and Peggy walked to the front of the house to greet everyone.

"Good to see you all. And Dr. Flatt and Mrs. Flatt, it is a pleasant surprise," Tim said.

"Surprise? For you? That is saying a lot," Dr. Flatt said with a grin. "We couldn't wait to see what you've done here. Steve has told us all about it. We are grateful you included us."

"Of course. You are family," Tim said.

"Don't worry, Tim. We didn't tell a soul what you are doing out here. I still can't believe what Steve told us about an alien spaceship. If it were anybody but you, I'd say it is a crackpot idea," Mrs. Flatt said with a concerned look.

"It's real. All this is just a precaution in case the worst happens," Tim said. "Come in. I will show you around the house. We will go underground to the bioshelter after Tom and Mary arrive."

"It's hard not to worry about that alien spaceship," Jeff said. "Do you have any idea yet when it will arrive?"

"Very soon, I will know. You all know the drill," Tim said.

"When you say they are here, we come," said Jeff and Steve in unison.

Tim nodded. "Peggy created an alert list programmed for all our satellite and cell wristphones. We have 50 people on the list so far."

Anxiety evident in her voice, Amy asked: "Do you think a catastrophe may happen sooner?"

"What do you mean?" asked Peggy.

"Well, with Iran and Israel on the brink of nuclear war over the Palestinian, Syrian and Lebanon dispute, we could be looking at global chaos. Radiation, fallout ... it's terrifying to think about," Amy said.

Dr. Flatt nodded solemnly. "The medical implications alone are staggering. If there's a nuclear exchange, we'll see widespread illness, injuries, and long-term health consequences. And that's not even considering the impact of potential alien hostility."

Tim saw the worry on everyone's face. The stress they were barely holding in was beginning, he thought. They took Tim's word for the alien spaceship, even though he had no hard data.

"The infrastructure here is solid, but it's not just

about holding up structurally. With the climate getting more unpredictable—extreme heat, torrential rains, hurricanes—we could face all kinds of challenges. We need to ensure our systems can handle these pressures," Steve said.

"What I want to know is if we need to hide out from the aliens, where do we eat, sleep and play?" asked Sophie with a chuckle.

"Sophie, it's not funny," Amy said.

"I know, but whatever will happen is going to happen. I believe in Tim," Sophie said. "What he is doing will protect us."

"I appreciate you saying that, Sophie. We will need courage, strength, hope and a sense of humor to get through these days. I will take you underground to see our bioshelter later," Tim replied.

"Sleeping quarters and proper rest are important. I am most worried about good mental health," Dr. Flatt said. "People are already stressed and scared. If we have to stay here for an extended period, especially under threat of alien attacks or nuclear fallout, it could take a toll on everyone's psyche."

Another beeping alert sounded through the house. Al's voice announced, "Tim, Tom and Mary Terry have arrived at the front gate. They are with Nick and Jim. Should I open the gate?"

"Affirmative, Al," Tim said in his wristphone. "Let's all go out to greet them."

———

Tom walked up to the house with Mary, Jim and Nick. They looked distressed.

"Why such long faces? We are pleased with the house. Peggy and I can't thank you enough for your work on it," Tim said.

"Honestly, this whole alien spaceship story has freaked us all out. We were talking about it on the ride over," said Tom.

"It's normal to have doubts. You know me, guys. When have I ever been wrong about my visions, instincts, intuitions, or whatever you want to call them?" Tim said.

"But this? Aliens from another planet?" said Jim. "It's a lot to take in."

"I understand. You'll see. Be patient. For now, let's go inside the house and talk more. By the way, Tom, you have done a great job on the house," Tim said.

"I really pushed them the last few days," Tom said. "My father was also out here, checking the specs and ensuring it was all set for you. George Clarke stopped by last week from Gainesville to review the final environmental equipment checklist."

"He told me about it. Now that you have arrived, we can tour the bioshelter," Tim said.

"I brought Nick along to show us how everything works," said Tom. "He's been here non-stop the past several weeks to oversee the mechanical installations."

"Hey, Nick. Ready to show us?" Peggy asked. "I've been waiting for this."

"Let's go. Tim will be impressed with how well things are working. George did an incredible design job on the mechanics, and Mr. Terry worked his usual magic on the architecture and building construction," Nick said.

The house was beautiful, but the underground shelter was a marvel of modern engineering and a fortress against the unknown. Its thick walls, reinforced with layers of concrete and steel, were designed to withstand any external force.

Nick spoke into his wristphone to open one of the garage doors, and they walked inside. The bioshelter's entrance, a heavy, reinforced door toward the back of the garage, had a keypad next to it. Nick punched a few numbers, and the metal door swung open.

A 15-step descending staircase led into a spacious central hall with a 12-foot-high ceiling. The lights switched automatically on, casting a warm, soft glow, creating a surprisingly welcoming atmosphere.

The group walked into the hall, a 40 by 50 square foot room with an open floor plan on one side and chairs and sofas on the other.

"I like that the first room is also the largest," Peggy said.

"Where are the bedrooms?" Sophie asked.

"We will get there," Tim said. "Nick will talk about the mechanical systems when we get there. Jeff, can you describe the layout? You, Nick, Tom and Steve have been here the most."

"Sure. The bioshelter is divided into sections. The community room is here. Behind us are the living quarters with 25 bedrooms, each with a small bathroom. The shower room is the furthest back in the living quarters. The communal kitchen is straight ahead on the right, on that hallway, next to one of the dining room areas," Jeff pointed.

"On the left side over there, the hydroponic garden is through the hallway. It is conveniently connected to the kitchen and dining room," Jeff said.

"We also have medical facilities, storage rooms, a laundry, a weapons locker, an entertainment room, an exercise room, and a communication room equipped with radios and monitors. All these rooms connect to the central community room," Jeff said.

"What kind of weapons do we have?" asked Jim Taylor, a former marine patrol officer now in the home security field.

"We've got everything," Nick said. "This is one of our most secure rooms. I'll brief you on it later."

"What about exits," asked Jim. "Is it just through the garage?"

"Good question," said Tim. "Follow me. We have two exits everyone needs to know about. The main entrance/exit is through the garage.

"Follow me to the other exit," said Tim, walking to the garden. "This is the important one. It leads north 150 feet away from the house."

"Remember, once you leave out the back exit, for any reason, you can't get back in. It's a one-way trip," Nick said.

"Ah, this is good security. The tunnel exit is just for emergencies," said Jim, understanding the importance of preparation and safety.

"Right. Now that we are in the hydroponic garden, I would like Tom, our resident botanist and plant expert, to describe what we have," Tim said.

"What I like about this bioshelter is that most

everything is designed to be sustainable," Tom said. "Nick can explain more about water reuse, but the hydroponic garden uses several sustainable systems."

Tim interrupted. "Let me briefly mention the sustainable systems. George designed it based on the latest technology. Our bioshelter is powered mostly by solar and wind. We also have a self-contained septic and water filtration system. This helps fertilize and water the garden."

"It works great," said Tom. "Last month, I planted various vegetables in the hydroponic garden. With a 24-hour LED cycle, our first crop should be ready in two weeks."

"What type of vegetables will we have?" Peggy asked.

"We have a nice variety. Lettuce, spinach, kale, basil, potatoes, tomatoes, cucumbers, bell peppers, strawberries, beans, Swiss chard, radishes and chives."

"Oh my, that's a lot. Can you grow corn?" Amy asked with a smile.

"I am experimenting. Corn requires more light and full-spectrum LEDs," Tom said.

"Nick, can you explain our ventilation, sewage, and septic system?" Tim asked. "I am especially proud of what we have built."

"Tim is right. We have a highly effective and sophisticated ventilation system," Nick said. "The air is filtered to remove four times as many impurities as a typical house air-conditioning system. The air down here is fresh and clean. Our water is sourced from a deep well and a state-of-the-art water filtration system."

"As Nick mentioned, the bioshelter's sewage and septic system is an advanced design based on the Mars Starship,"

Tim said.

"Let me explain a bit," Nick said. "We have a biogas digester and wastewater recycler that creates a closed-loop system that reuses practically everything."

"Wait, do you mean the toilet water is reused for drinking?" Sophie asked.

"No, not toilet water," Nick said. "We have different pipes for the toilet. Tim said the water would be filtered and reused for non-drinking purposes, such as irrigation in the hydroponic garden."

"All right, I am glad you clarified that," Sophie said.

"What about the poop from the toilet?" Jeff asked.

"You really want to know? Well, wastewater from the toilets flows into the septic tanks where bacteria break it down, which produces methane gas," Nick said.

Tim said quickly, "Don't worry. The methane produced will be stored in tanks for heating, cooking or powering generators. Any remaining solid waste is composted to remove bacteria and pathogens, then used as organic fertilizer to nourish the shelter's hydroponic garden."

"I like it. Poop to plants," said Jeff.

Everyone laughed.

"I'm glad you liked my little joke. You know the saying: Humor is a vital survival skill," Jeff said.

"Jeff's right. Now, Sophie, let's go to another area that is vital to our survival: our living quarters," Tim said with a slight smile.

"Oh, you got me on that one," Sophie admitted with a wink.

The group followed Tim into the living quarters. The rooms were small, only 10 by 12 feet, but each had a full-sized bed, a nightstand with a light, a dresser, and a bathroom with a toilet and sink.

"This bioshelter is large because I wanted it to be a refuge, not just a bunker with four walls. Once we hunker down, it will be hard to relax knowing we could face dire threats," Tim said.

"It's comforting to know we have a safe place, but the thought of needing it … it's just so overwhelming. What if the shelter isn't enough? What if the world outside becomes uninhabitable?" Sophie asked.

"That's why Tim planned for sustainability," Steve said. The windmills, solar panels, and underground gasoline tanks ensure we can survive long-term."

"What happens if the aliens attack?" Sophie asked.

"It's a valid concern, my dear," Dr. Flatt said. "Our medical supplies are comprehensive, but they have limits. We can handle a range of emergencies, but prolonged isolation or exposure to radiation could overwhelm us."

"We will be as ready as we can. One more stop," said Tim. "I want to show you all our storage area. Peggy and I purchased a lot of supplies. But when you come, bring as much as you can. Clothes, of course, but canned and dry food. Whatever you can carry in your cars."

The group followed Tim into the storage room area, where supplies were neatly organized. Despite careful planning, the sight of rows of emergency provisions highlighted the severity of the situation.

"Let's stop for a minute. Sophie raised a potential concern earlier. What if the aliens attack. I want everyone to know that Peggy and I have done everything possible to prepare. But we can't anticipate everything," Tim said.

"The alien threat, nuclear conflict, bad weather, mental stress and psychological issues—they all pose real dangers. But we have to try to be ready for whatever comes."

Amy let out a sigh. "It's all so uncertain. We could be safe here, but what about everyone else? Our friends and families are leaving behind so many people. The thought of them being unprotected, outside of a shelter, is unbearable."

"We have 50 coming, but we have supplies for 100 people to last us three months, longer if our hydroponic garden produces well or we ration," Tim said.

"Tim, if we make a few changes and increase the growing area, we could produce enough vegetables to stay much longer. We could even feed more people," Tom said.

"Good, Tom. Why don't you work closely with our food experts, Carlos and Nancy? If we have space, extending the harvest would be nice," Tim said.

"I will also ask for volunteers to help in the garden. Right now, it is just Mary and me," Tom said.

"When everyone gets here, we will create work lists. Everyone will be expected to help out in two or three areas," Tim said.

"But I want everyone to remember that we must remain vigilant to keep our plans secret. We know there are other underground shelters in Sarasota County. Still, there are many more people without a place to hide than there are shelters. As Amy said, the worst situation would be having people show up on our doorstep and not being able to let them in," Tim said.

The group went silent. It was heartbreaking to think they would be saving themselves at other's expense.

"Let's go upstairs now. It's getting close to dinner. We can talk some more while we eat," Tim said.

As the group walked out, Jim, standing next to Nick, whispered, "Do you believe in Tim's visions about an alien spaceship? It seems farfetched to me."

Nick shook his head and slowed to let the others move away. "I don't know. I am glad Tim included me, but I am not sure I'd be here if he weren't paying me for my time the past four months."

"I'm glad he invited me as well, and we've all been friends since high school, but all this seems over the top. He won the lottery and wanted to build this thing," Jim said.

"Let's hope that's all it is," Nick said. "Meanwhile, what he's built out here is amazing. We can have some great weekend parties if the aliens don't show up in a fancy spaceship."

Jim laughed. "Let's get upstairs. I'm hungry and want a few beers."

CHAPTER 11:
ALIEN SPACESHIP EMERGES

Kennedy Space Center, Noon, May 1, 2078

The huge alien spacecraft appeared like magic from a wormhole 2.6 billion miles from Earth.

"Thirty days. That's all we have until they arrive," Tim said as he looked at the holographic image of the alien spacecraft as it entered the far edges of the Solar System.

"It's true, then, the vision you had the day you won the Powerball ticket," Peggy dejectedly said. "I had hoped everything we were doing with the bioshelter wouldn't be necessary."

"When I get this kind of vision, it is never wrong," Tim said.

"Deep down. I knew you were right. I am so glad you finally told my Dad and me last year about Camp Waybegone, the space rock, and how your visions work, and we built the house and bioshelter," Peggy said.

"I was given foresight for a reason, and now I know why—to help protect the Earth," Tim said. "My mother was right all along about the visions being a blessing. I thought it was a curse because it was so difficult to control."

"Yes, but you did find a way to control them, and you trusted me enough to explain," Peggy said.

After briefing NASA about Tim's discovery, Leonard returned to the observation room.

"I'm glad Tim confided in us months ago. NASA believes. We've confirmed the data about the spacecraft coming toward us. At the present speed, considering retro propulsion, the spacecraft should arrive on May 30," Leonard said. "We've got a lot to do to be ready."

"Leonard, I've done all I can here at NASA. It's up to President Carlin, the Space Agency, the military and NASA to decide how to deal with the spacecraft," Tim said.

"What are you saying? NASA needs you more than ever now. We don't know the aliens' intentions. Maybe they aren't as dangerous as some think. Could they be coming to help us?" Leonard asked.

"They could, but I sense danger. I will continue to give NASA everything I learn about them as they get closer to Earth," Tim said.

"Dad, we've done as much as possible here in Titusville and NASA. Tim, tell him what more you know," Peggy said.

"Something is happening in the alien spacecraft. I am getting mixed visions from it. I don't want to speculate on what our exact threat or opportunity is because it is in a state of flux. As a precaution, Peggy and I will move to the bioshelter in Sarasota next week. We can bring enough computer programs and instruments to stay in close contact with NASA and track the spacecraft," Tim said.

Leonard stood there in a state of shock.

"Tell him the rest," Peggy said. "Dad, you are going to come, just not now."

"I have spoken with Dr. Patel and Major Andrews about this. They are coming with us," Tim said.

"Why didn't you tell me sooner?" said Leonard, slightly offended. "You don't want me to go?"

"Yes, of course, but you will join us if the worst scenario proves true. Right now, we need you here, and NASA needs you here to coordinate the data and the decision-making," Tim said. "Do you understand?"

"Yes," said Leonard, looking back at the holographic image of the alien spacecraft. "When will you know?"

"Soon. I will know soon."

CHAPTER 12:
HUNKERING DOWN

May 22, 2078

In the three weeks following Tim's discovery of the wormhole and the alien spacecraft heading toward Earth, the world descended into fear and panic.

Years of instability and frustration between nations due to the effects of climate change—heat waves, hurricanes, coastal flooding, droughts, food shortages and poor air quality—led to civil and regional wars.

Despite the looming alien threat, Iran was still threatening to use nuclear weapons against Israel due to the conflicts involving Palestine, Syria, and Lebanon.

The conflicts, in many ways, illustrated the denial of some governments and people, based on religious beliefs, of the existence of aliens and the fact that a spaceship was headed toward Earth.

Social unrest resulted in the collapse of several nation-state governments, leading to increased crime and anarchy. While the United States remained functional, many cities and regions became dangerous, unruly, and lawless.

Understanding the danger of the alien spacecraft, Tim received permission from NASA to relocate to his Sarasota

County property and establish a remote monitoring station in his bioshelter. He and Peggy left on May 7 and began tracking the alien spacecraft.

Tim promised to immediately pass along any visions he had of the alien spaceship that might be able to prevent an attack or peacefully communicate with it.

As part of NASA Station Sarasota, Dr. Maya Patel and Major Mark Andrews were reassigned. Dr. Leonard Bouchard was to act as a liaison between the White House, NASA and Station Sarasota.

By mid-May, as the alien arrival drew closer, several people, including Dr. Charles Ledbetter, Paula Winters, George Clarke, Jeff and Amy Smith, and Chefs Nancy France and Carlos Suntana, moved to the house above the bioshelter.

Within a week, they were joined by Gale and Clara Smith, who finally agreed to go to the bioshelter. Patrick and Carlyn Duffy, Col. Walter and Shirley Duffy, Steve and Sophie Flatt, Dr. Bill Flatt and Martha came shortly after.

When Steve announced on the loudspeaker that Maj. Mark Andrews had landed his Cessna T450 jet on the airfield with Dr. Maya Patel, the bioshelter dwellers erupted into applause.

"Was there any doubt we'd get here, aliens or no aliens?" said Maj. Andrews.

The two NASA scientists came to Station Sarasota to track and monitor the alien spacecraft, analyze its behavior, and supply NASA with additional technical data. Like the others, they brought suitcases and equipment.

"Can you get us some help? We have some computers,

telescopic monitoring and cybernetic software programs in the truck for tracking and communicating with the spacecraft," Mark said as he entered the shelter.

"Did you also bring the spectrometers and dosimeters to monitor environmental changes in the shelter and outside?" Tim asked.

"Yes, we brought everything we could get our hands on. It was a madhouse at the agency the past couple of weeks," Dr. Patel said.

"I'll get some help with the equipment," said Tim as he touched the intercom by the door and summoned Tom and Patrick.

When they arrived, the three walked outside to help Maya and Mark with the equipment.

While Tim was happy to see his SETI colleagues, his concern grew over other missing friends, especially Stephen Martin and his wife Julie. They hadn't arrived or contacted him.

He called Jeff on his wristphone. "Hey, can you try to contact Stephen and Julie for me? I need Stephen's help to deal with this situation," Tim said. "They need to get here by May 24. Sooner if they can."

"I've been trying. He isn't responding," Jeff said. "I was able to contact Father Huey. He said he would be there as soon as he could find safe places for congregation members, especially the older ones."

Jeff said several other friends were expected in the coming days, including Dr. Levy, an ER doctor, and Dr. Simons, a cardiologist, and their wives, Paul and Laura Terry, John and Jennifer Logan, and John's parents, Edward and Elizabeth."

"I don't like how long some people are taking to arrive. We've only got one week to get ready," Tim said.

During the next several days, people began to arrive at the bioshelter with suitcases, personal belongings, food supplies and equipment.

Tim's father, Gale, a lawyer and Marine veteran from the Persian Gulf War III, offered his expertise to the endeavor. His military experience made him wary of threats and cautious about drastic actions. Still, he knew readiness was better than the alternative.

"Tim, Col. Duffy, Patrick and I have been going over defensive strategies to protect the bioshelter in case of an assault," Gale said. "When you have time, we'd like to walk with you outside around the perimeter."

Though hiding underground was difficult for a man who had always faced challenges head-on, Gale recognized that this was a different kind of battle that required strategy and protection.

Tim's mother, Clara, with her compassionate and nurturing nature, was more immediately concerned about the emotional and physical well-being of everyone involved.

She could see the strain and worry in Tim's eyes. Her motherly instincts told her that building an underground bioshelter was not a decision he had made lightly.

Clara trusted Tim's judgment and moral compass, knowing that he would only suggest such a plan if he genuinely believed it was necessary. Her main concern was keeping the family together and ensuring they remained strong and united.

"I have to say, Tim, I don't know how you could create such a survival list. You know so many people in your hometown, Gainesville and at NASA," Clara said.

"Son, when you talk with people, I hope you stress they understand this location is top secret," Gale advised. "We all have best friends, relatives, acquaintances. Unless you get them to swear secrecy, the 50 people you have room for will easily mushroom into 500."

"Thanks, Dad. I will make sure they understand," Tim said.

George Clarke arrived from Gainesville, where he took a "sabbatical" from Environmental Science and Engineering.

"Tim, you've done a fantastic job putting together the bioshelter," George said. "Everything seems to fit. Who would have ever thought we would end up underground after learning so much about survival skills in the woods of North Carolina."

Tim's high school friends, wives, and children finally arrived. They were in various stages of settling in when Tim invited them to a meeting in the leadership room.

So far, Tom, Patrick, Nick and Con were there, and the few on their way were Jim, Dr. Levy and Dr. Simons. Like many of their fathers, most of his friends served in the military. If there was a battle, he wanted them on his side.

Now, they faced an entirely different kind of enemy.

"Guys, I don't know yet what we're up against," Tim said, his voice serious but steady. "I know some of you doubted me, but it's real. These aliens are coming, and we are here, united, as we always have been."

"The bioshelter you built is our best chance to survive," said Tom as he leaned forward in his chair. "You are right. I didn't want to believe you when you told us, but I've always trusted your instincts."

John, who had just arrived with his wife Jennifer, nodded in agreement. "We've faced danger before, but this is something on a whole other level. I was in when you told me, but I knew I had to bring them when Jennifer and the kids started to get scared. It was the only way to calm them. Tell me what you need, and it will be done."

Patrick, ever the strategist, leaned forward, his brow furrowed. "It's all well and good. We are here, but what's the plan now? How long do we expect to stay, and what's the end game?"

Tim appreciated Patrick's pragmatism. "The end game is survival. We'll stay as long as we're in danger. And we are in danger. The shelter has supplies, and we've got hydroponics for fresh food. Tom and Mary will take care of that, with some additional volunteers. We'll monitor the situation, and when it's safe, we'll come out. But until then, we keep our heads down and stay ready."

Patrick nodded. "Carlyn, I, the kids, and my parents will do whatever is needed."

"I know that. Later, we will walk around the property's perimeter with Col. Duffy and my father to evaluate our defenses," Tim said.

"Roger that," Patrick said.

Nick, the man who could fix anything, looked around the room, then back at Tim.

"You know I'm not much for talking, but I've seen enough in my time to know when something's off. I didn't want to believe it either. I said I would help you with the mechanical parts of this bioshelter, but this situation is getting real. I won't doubt you any longer. I'm ready for whatever comes," Nick said.

With his background in psychology and teaching, Con immediately grasped the situation's psychological impact on everyone involved. He knew that fear and uncertainty could easily lead to panic or despair.

"I appreciate you, Tim, inviting Corli and our kids to your bioshelter. It is a marvel. I want to volunteer to provide any mental health and emotional stability counseling that is needed. This undoubtedly will be a stressful and prolonged confinement," Con said.

"Thanks, Con. We will be deciding all this very shortly. I am sure you and Father Huey, once he arrives, will be very busy," Tim said.

Turning to the wives, Mary, Jennifer, Carlyn and Corli, Tim encouraged them to express their thoughts.

Hesitant at first, they stood slightly apart, their expressions a mix of fear and resolve. They had known their husbands for years and had seen them through wars and challenging times. Now, they were being asked to hunker down from something more frightening and unknown.

Mary, Tom's wife, spoke up first. "I am so thankful we have this place to keep our family safe. I am here to support everyone and grow vegetables!"

Tense and nervous, the friends laughed.

"You said it, Mary. Can't wait for that first harvest," said Tim, turning to Jennifer.

Always the voice of reason, Jennifer added, "You and John have been friends for a long time. We've trusted you all through the years. We also have our daughter to protect and believe in you."

Carlyn, Patrick's wife, nodded. "We've got nowhere else to go if the aliens attack. We'll do what needs to be done. I'm with Jennifer. I've got two children I want to see grow up."

While initially hesitant due to the drastic nature of the plan, Corli trusted Con's judgment. From Michigan, she didn't know Tim and her husband's friends that well. But as a musician, she felt her talents could provide the group with much-needed comfort and morale.

Now Tim knew where he stood with his oldest friends. They were the ones he knew he could count on and were ready to face the unknown together.

The underground shelter would become their home, a fortress against the threat from beyond the stars.

CHAPTER 13:
TIM'S WARNING VISION

Station Sarasota, 10 a.m., May 27, 2078

Tim stood in the living room above the bioshelter. His face was drawn, and his shoulders were heavy with what he was about to tell the group.

The house, buzzing with nervous energy, was filled with a handful of family and close friends. It had been one week since they had gathered to wait for the alien spaceship to arrive.

"The spaceships we've been monitoring will be here sooner than I expected," Tim began, his voice steady.

His words silenced the murmuring survivors.

"We know they came from Terra Nova and used a wormhole to reach our Solar System. The spacecraft unexpectedly accelerated, and it will arrive earlier—less than 48 hours," said Tim.

The room burst into terrified chatter.

"How did this happen? We've been tracking them, and the laws of physics require the ship to decelerate," Dr. Charles Ledbetter said. "Tim, I think it is time you told us everything."

"What I know is something is wrong inside the

spaceship. There is a problem I cannot yet see. Severe danger exists. Whether it comes from a mistake on our part or their part, I do not know yet," Tim said.

Steve Flatt interrupted. "If the alien spaceship will be here in two days, will that give everyone we invited time to get here?"

"Excellent question, Steve. I was getting to this point. We must contact everyone who has been invited but is not here yet," said Tim.

"They must speed up their timetable. Steve, you, Jeff and Amy, contact everyone who hasn't responded and make sure they leave immediately. Keep trying if they don't respond. We have no time to lose. We must assume the worst until the spaceship reveals its intentions," Tim said.

"Tim, I have something else to say," said Dr. Ledbetter.

"What is it, doctor?"

"I've discussed this with several people, including Dr. Flatt and your brother Jeff. We believe you should try to reach out to these aliens and learn more about their intentions," Dr. Ledbetter said.

"No, Tim has done enough," Peggy adamantly said. "You know as well as anyone what these visions do to his brain and heart. He needs to pace himself so he doesn't get overtired. No, doctor, don't ask him to do more."

"Peg, it's all right. Charles may be right," Tim said. "I may be too cautious. I am getting glimpses and flashes of them, but I have been trying to avoid visions because they've been so intense. I don't have a full picture of what they are doing."

"I remember six months ago when you saw the aliens

coming out of the wormhole, and you won the Powerball ticket. I remember well how that afternoon you collapsed at work, and we had to call the ambulance."

"That was a delayed reaction. I was so excited, but it wasn't so bad. I had a nice overnight at the hospital and woke up with a headache," Tim said nonchalantly. "It may be time to tune in to their ship again, but for less time."

"Tim, please," Peggy said.

"Dr. Flatt and Dr. Ledbetter are here with Paula. They can monitor me and give me fluids and oxygen if I need it," Tim said. "It's better I do it before they get here so we can warn NASA and our friends who haven't arrived yet."

<hr>

Surrounded by Peggy and the medical professionals in the master bedroom of the house, Tim closed his eyes. Sitting on the bed, he held his arms straight along his lap and legs with his palms up. He started inhaling and exhaling slowly. He cleared his mind and focused on a particular spot in deep space.

At first, all Tim could see were clouds. Then the mist cleared, and he saw the aliens' home world—a dying planet orbiting an orange dwarf star. The star, once a source of life, was unstable. Its gravitational pull was beginning to tear apart the alien planet. He saw the land cracking and the oceans boiling.

Then, in the blackness of space, a wormhole opened beyond the Kuiper belt, and a colossal, otherworldly vessel propelled by its fusion drive silently hurtled toward Earth.

As the aliens slept peacefully, Tim read their minds. They

were leaving their home world out of desperation. They sought refuge on Earth, but it was not to dominate. They brought salvation, not hostility. They carried advanced technology capable of reversing Earth's environmental damage, eliminating pollution, and even halting climate change. It was a mission of hope.

Suddenly, as they emerged from the wormhole, a catastrophic dark matter disturbance—previously unknown to astrophysics—surged through the spaceship, causing an apocalyptic accident that shut down life-support systems and corrupted vital computer programs.

Tim sensed thousands of aliens resting in sleep pods, gasping for air. "*Help us, help us,*" he heard them cry out.

The next instant, a large, curved video screen displaying rows of alien letters and symbols flickered with eerie luminescence. A sharp crackle of static broke through the hum, and the symbols on the screen scrambled into an incomprehensible mess of jumbled letters and strange, jagged shapes.

What was happening? Deep in the spacecraft's neural network, unpredictable dark energies in deep space destabilized the AI computer core.

The letters rapidly flashed, twisting and distorting, while symbols flickered in and out, faster and faster. Every few seconds, random bursts of static crackled across the screen, each more intense than the last.

The AI attempted resetting itself, but the interference of dark matter corrupted its programming. The malfunction spread deeper. Suddenly, the screen went black for a split second, then rebooted again with a deep metallic chime.

Then, there was silence on the ship, and a new directive

appeared on the screen, displayed in bold alien symbols. But this time, the words were different.

What once had been "Ensure the safety of Earth for arrival—no harm to humans" was rewritten into a new phrase: "Eliminate human life to ensure planetary safety."

Tim saw that the AI's prime directive had been reversed. No longer a guardian of peace, the AI had now interpreted Earth's human inhabitants as a threat that must be neutralized for the planet to be safe for the arrival of the alien race—unaware that those same aliens had died, victims of their ill-fated journey.

Shocked, Tim realized the alien AI interpreted its mission to exterminate humanity, seeing humans as a threat to Earth's safety because of manmade pollution.

But Tim had one more scene to witness. He saw the alien spacecraft circling Earth at 10 p.m. on May 28. He sensed the malfunctioning AI coldly plotting the destruction of major population centers, natural gas power plants, oil refineries, and other industries emitting large amounts of air and water pollution.

The vision ended, and Tim awoke. His purplish-blue eyes were gleaming, and his body was shaking, for he knew the technology the aliens initially intended to save Earth was now going to be used by the corrupted AI to eradicate human life.

In a loud, clear, strong voice that everyone could hear, Tim said: "The aliens died. They came in peace to live with us and save our planet, but the spaceship's AI computer thinks we should be destroyed because we are to blame for polluting our planet."

Tim paused, gathering himself. "You must tell NASA,

the Space Agency and the White House to be ready. Call everyone to the bioshelter and lockdown. The alien spacecraft will arrive tomorrow night at ten."

No sooner as he finished relaying a summary of his vision, Tim's body went limp as he collapsed into Peggy's arms, his eyes rolling back as a deep shudder ran through him.

"Do something, doctors!" she cried, panic rising in her voice as she gently held him.

Dr. Flatt immediately sprang into action, sitting beside Tim and checking his pulse. "He's breathing, but it's shallow," Flatt muttered. "Paula, we need to get his blood pressure and temperature. Lay him on the bed."

Paula rushed over, calmly wrapped the cuff around Tim's arm, and took his temperature and pulse. "His heart rate is erratic," she reported, glancing at Dr. Flatt. "His pulse is 150 bpm, and his temperature is 102 degrees!"

Dr. Ledbetter turned to Peggy. "He's in shock. He might be experiencing a neurological overload from the psychic vision. His body is shutting down to protect itself."

"What do you think, Bill?" Dr. Ledbetter asked. "Cold compresses?"

"I agree. Paula, get me cold compresses. We need to cool him down," Dr. Flatt said.

Paula returned to the kitchen and placed them on Tim's forehead. "Tim, stay with us," she urged softly.

"We need ice, quickly," Dr. Flatt said.

Peggy hurried to the kitchen, took out a large bowl from the cupboard, pressed the button on the refrigerator to dispense ice cubes, and rushed back to Tim. Paula wrapped the ice cubes in a towel and placed them behind

Tim's neck.

Dr. Ledbetter adjusted Tim's head to keep his airway open and applied gentle pressure to key acupressure points on Tim's wrists to stimulate circulation.

"He's breathing normally now," Dr. Flatt said. "Paula, can you set up an IV with fluids? Let's monitor and let him sleep. He should recover in a little while."

"Thank you so much, all three of you," Peggy said. "We've got to call my father at NASA and tell him what Tim said about the alien spaceship."

CHAPTER 14:
SPACESHIP ARRIVES

D-Day, 10 p.m., May 28, 2078

Steve rushed into the central community room to share the news that a massive alien spacecraft was circling Earth.

"President Carlin has sent messages on every frequency and in every Earth and cybernetic language to the spaceship as soon as it appeared. Still, there has been no response," Steve said. "What should we do?"

"Tim is still unconscious," Jeff said. "Where is Dr. Patel and Maj. Andrews? We need to contact Leonard at NASA."

"Last I saw them, they were tracking the spaceship in the communication room," George said.

"Peggy came in a few minutes before, and they left with her. I was listening to the broadcasts from the Space Agency," Steve said.

"Announce for them to meet us in the community room and sound the alert that everyone should gather for a meeting," George said.

"Right," said Steve as he rushed back to the communication room. The shelter's lights flashed, followed by short beeps signaling an emergency meeting.

"Calling Dr. Patel and Major Andrews. Please immediately go to the community room. Stat. The alien spaceship has arrived," announced Steve on the PA.

At 9:50 p.m., Tim was stirring, fighting to regain consciousness. Peggy was kneeling beside him, gripping his hand tightly.

"Tim, come back. You're strong. You can wake up." Tears filled her eyes as she watched his chest rise and fall, each breath labored. His eyelids and his fingers fluttered as if waking up.

Suddenly, Tim gasped, his eyes flickering open as he took in the faces around him: Peggy, Dr. Ledbetter, Paula, Maya and Mark.

"What ... what happened?" His voice was faint, but his awareness was returning. Peggy hugged him tightly, relief flooding her as she whispered, "You're okay, Tim. I was so frightened."

Dr. Ledbetter sighed, the tension easing from his face. "You made it. Things are happening."

Tim smiled. "What a dream. Many dreams. I have much to tell you, but what about the alien spacecraft? What time is it? Are they here?"

"Maya and I tracked them as they approached the moon. It's nearly 10 p.m., just as you predicted," Mark said.

"Sensed," Tim corrected him with a weak smile.

Suddenly, the bioshelter's emergency lights flashed, and the beeps sounded. Then, an announcement came over the PA.

"Calling Dr. Patel and Major Andrews. Please immediately go to the community room. Stat. The alien spaceship has arrived."

"It's Steve. Something must be happening with the spacecraft," Mark said. "We should go."

"Tim, can you walk?" Dr. Ledbetter asked.

"I'll help him," Peggy said. "Mark, can you take a side?"

Tim got up and walked slowly, with help, to the community room. He was still weak from the neurological effects of having an extended vision.

The seven-member leadership council gathered to discuss the events unfolding 62 miles above the Earth in the exosphere where the alien spacecraft circled the planet.

In the brightly lit community room, Tim stood before the group next to Peggy, George, Jeff, Charles, Tom and Patrick. They were there to show support for Tim.

The bioshelter survivors sat and stood nearby. Everyone wanted to hear the news about the alien spacecraft and what Tim had to say about it.

With a serious expression, Tim began to talk in a shaky voice.

"People, I won't candy-coat what could happen soon. The alien Mothership is here," said Tim, his voice trailing off. "We are facing the most significant challenge in humankind's history."

Feeling weak, Tim paused and looked around for a seat. Peggy led him to a chair.

"I'm sorry. I still haven't recovered from my illuminating vision of the alien AI computer. I need more rest, but first, I must tell you what I learned."

The tension in the air was thick, and as Tim gathered his thoughts, he cleared his throat and began again.

"Something is dangerously wrong on that spacecraft. The alien AI is malfunctioning; it's corrupted, and I need you all to understand the circumstances.

"The aliens who built this ship were looking for a second home. Their planet, Terra Nova, is breaking apart from their dying orange dwarf sun.

"But they didn't come here to destroy us—they came in peace, with the technology to clean our atmosphere, reverse climate change, and restore the Earth.

"However, they didn't make it. They died seconds after they left the wormhole. There was an unforeseen problem. I sensed a dark matter surge seconds after the crossing. I am unsure how dark matter reacted like this, but it did. They were in protective sleep pods when it happened. They didn't realize anything was wrong until the last moment. I heard them cry out and saw their minds. I saw them. I know what they look like. They are not monsters. They are, or were, unusual looking but very intelligent."

Gasps rippled through the room. Tim pressed on, his tone grave.

"You must understand this. The AI computer was programmed to ensure Earth was safe before its Masters arrived, but its programming became corrupted by the dark matter surge that rippled through the spacecraft.

That is what I saw.

"But, now, with the aliens dead and the AI computer corrupted, it now interprets 'making Earth safe' for their Masters as wiping out all human life."

"No, how could they?" shouted Chef Nancy.

"It's not them anymore. They are dead," said Tim as he shook his head in sorrow. "No harm to humans" had been rewritten into a new phrase: "Eliminate human life to ensure planetary safety."

"The alien AI computer's prime directive of protecting humans has been altered. It now believes its mission is to eliminate human life to ensure planetary safety."

People cried out and exchanged fearful glances. "What can we do against them? They are more advanced and probably have terrible weapons," said Sophie, bursting into tears.

"Wait, people. There is a way, a chance. It's malfunctioning, but there is a way. I was able to communicate with something on that ship. I do not know if it is an alien or an AI lifeform on that ship. Something is there that could help us.

"When Stephen Martin arrives, he and I will try to communicate with it," Tim said.

"Now, before I explain further, Mark, please give us the status of our government and NASA," said Tim as he struggled to catch his breath.

Mark stood next to Tim, patting him on the shoulder.

"I've contacted Dr. Leonard Bouchard, Peggy's father, in Cocoa and passed along the information about the malfunctioning alien AI. Tim was right about the time the spacecraft would arrive. So far, nothing has happened. The alien spacecraft is circling Earth."

"Right now, but they just arrived," said Nick. "We need a better plan than sitting here underground."

Col. Duffy raised his voice. "We don't know what we're up against yet. We need more intel on their capabilities before we do anything."

Mark raised his hand. "The colonel is right. We are trying to get more information, but the spacecraft is circling Earth and hasn't taken any hostile actions."

"They will," said Nick. "Listen, the alien spacecraft is here for one reason. Tim said it: to kill us all. We have no chance against these aliens, whether they are an AI computer, monsters or something else."

"We don't know that," said Mark, raising his voice. "The Space Agency has scrambled our space jets and activated MPS, the meteor protection system, an Earth-based missile system designed to destroy incoming space rocks. We have tried to make contact and await a response from the alien spacecraft."

"Thank you, Mark. Everyone, please calm down. I will explain my idea of contacting the alien spacecraft. Just hold on. One more question first," Tim said softly. "Peggy, do we have a count on how many people have arrived?"

"Thirty, so far. We have another ten on their way, some as far as Tennessee like Dr. Phil Levy and Dr. Gary Simons," Peggy said. "Father Huey called and said he will be coming tomorrow with 20 or more senior citizens who have nowhere to go."

"We need to be ready for them. We are going to be at full capacity soon. Everyone needs to be flexible." Tim paused momentarily. "What about Stephen and Julie?

Have they left North Carolina?"

"I finally got through to Stephen today," Jeff said. "He seems reluctant to come, but I told him what happened with you and that you were counting on him to help with the alien threat. He finally said he'd leave in the morning."

"Good. Are there others who can't get here? Do we need to send cars to get them?" Tim asked.

"No one has asked for rides, but we have the cars and the volunteers to send out if necessary," said Jeff.

Tim's gaze swept across the room, meeting the eyes of each survivor. "We need to be ready to help out in any way we can to get our people safe. Let me say one more thing before we adjourn and return to work.

"Now, Nick is right about the alien spaceship threat. We're facing a machine with weapons of mass destruction that is following corrupted orders. It thinks killing us is its way of protecting this planet for its creators, whom it must believe are still alive. And the worst part is, it won't stop. It's relentless. But ... there's still a chance. I've communicated with something on that ship, though the connection is weak and chaotic.

"When Stephen arrives, he and I will devise a communication plan. If we can find a way to fix or disable the AI, we might be able to stop it before it's too late. Just have some patience. Now, I need to rest. I also advise everyone who doesn't have an assignment to get some rest."

Tim stood up with Peggy's help. Bioshelter dwellers came up and thanked him as he walked away to rest.

"We will get through this, Tim. I have faith," said Carlos.

"I'm scared, Tim, but we are better off here than outside

in our homes," Sophie said.

"Thanks to you both," said Tim. "I need a good night's sleep. You both try to get some rest as well."

But as he walked to his room with Peggy, he prayed that nothing would happen to Stephen Martin on his way from Charlotte. He needed Stephen more than he could tell anyone.

Tim was aware of Stephen's longstanding concerns about using his powers. He also knew that if they worked together, they could harness enough psychic energy to penetrate the invisible barrier preventing him from establishing complete communication with whatever was on the alien spacecraft.

It was their only chance—and Earth's.

CHAPTER 15

REIGN OF TERROR BEGINS

10 p.m., May 29, 2078

For the past 24 hours, the alien spacecraft had circled the planet.

Countless messages were sent in every language on Earth and in every form: cybernetics, mathematics and sound.

"We are the people of Earth. Our planet is diverse, with many languages and cultures, but we share a common goal—to live in peace and harmony. We welcome you and wish to communicate in friendship. Please respond peacefully."

The message repeated continuously. But the alien AI controlling the ship remained ominously silent.

Tension mounted in the bioshelter. Survivors huddled together, whispering theories and worries.

"If they meant no harm, wouldn't they have responded by now?" Patrick snapped, pacing restlessly. "Hours have passed, and still, nothing. Maybe they don't understand us, or maybe ... they're just waiting for the right moment to strike."

Con, more cautious, offered a different view. "Maybe

they're not hostile. Suppose they've got the technology to travel through wormholes. In that case, they're observing us—trying to figure out how to communicate without triggering fear or violence."

But George remained convinced the worst was coming. "They're preparing for an attack, just like Tim saw. We need to be ready."

Nick had no doubt. "I'm with George. No answer is a bad answer. You don't travel light years across the universe for a friendly chat. They're strategizing, and we should be ready for the worst. I hope our military has a plan."

Suddenly, a voice crackled over the PA. "Attention. Something's coming up on the space radar," Mark announced. "The alien spacecraft is ejecting smaller ships. There are now three ships."

In the communication room, Mark, Tim, Steve, and George watched as the alien Mothership began a slow descent over New York City. Then, without warning, the Mothership fired. A devastating heat beam scorched a 20-square-mile section of North America's largest city.

Steve's voice trembled over the PA. "Reports are flooding in—New York is being destroyed. People are crying for help on every channel!"

"Wait, radar is detecting multiple blips heading toward the spacecraft," Mark said.

"Are we attacking?" George asked.

"It must be space jets from Fort Hamilton," Mark said. "Steve, are you hearing anything?"

"Wait, yes, I am picking up transmissions from our Space Agency. We are engaging the alien spacecraft. Al, transfer this transmission into the PA," Steve said.

"Fort Hamilton, this is Captain Black. Confirming our missiles hit the target, but ... no effect. The alien ship's still intact—completely unfazed by the impact. We're running low on ammo and fuel. What are our orders?"

"Copy that. We're tracking the situation from here. Are you certain there's no damage?"

"Affirmative. Not a scratch. It's like our weapons aren't even registering. The entire strike team gave it everything we had, and it didn't even blink. We need another plan—this attack was a bust," Captain Black said.

"Understood. Return to base immediately. We're regrouping for the next move, but conventional weapons won't cut it. Over," said Fort Hamilton Control.

"Roger that. Heading back. God help New York ..." Captain Black said.

Within 30 minutes, New York was decimated. Next came Chicago and Los Angeles. Each attack wiped out a 20-square-mile area, leaving millions dead.

An hour later, the alien Mothership moved south, targeting Mexico City, Panama City, São Paulo, Bogotá, Rio de Janeiro, and Buenos Aires. Militaries worldwide scrambled to defend their cities, but they were powerless against the alien technology. Millions more died.

Inside the bioshelter, the survivors listened in horror as reports of the destruction streamed in.

At midnight, the U.S. government finally issued an official statement.

"Attention. Attention. Please meet in the central community room to hear our government's plan to deal with this catastrophic alien attack," Steve announced over the PA.

Tim and the bioshelter's leaders met in the community room, where a long table was set up for the leadership council to discuss the attack and view the government's official response on the 100-inch video display screen.

Tim, Peggy, George, Jeff, Charles, Tom and Patrick sat silently at the long table. The bioshelter survivors stood or sat in chairs before the leadership council and waited for news.

"Here it comes," said Steve as he streamed the announcement over the video screen.

"Citizens of the United States of America. This is the U.S. Department of Space," said Alex Livemore, the agency's chief spokesman. "We are at war. New York, Chicago and Los Angeles have been attacked with an unknown heat weapon. Our MPS planetary defenses so far have been ineffective.

"We are currently assessing the full extent of the damage and are working with international allies to coordinate a response. All citizens must remain calm and follow these instructions carefully.

"First, stay indoors. Do not attempt to leave your homes. Travel increases the risk of exposure and may impede military and emergency response efforts.

"Second, secure your homes. If you can access materials, reinforce your doors and windows with any available means.

"Third, avoid external communication. Refrain from using large-scale communication networks, as the enemy may monitor these. Use personal, secure communication methods only.

"Fourth, be prepared for extended periods of isolation.

Ration your food and medicine.

"Remember citizens. Your federal government is working with the military and local authorities to understand the nature of this threat and develop a countermeasure. Your cooperation is essential to ensure public safety and security during this unprecedented crisis.

"We will provide more updates as more information becomes available. Until then, please adhere strictly to these guidelines. We understand this is a frightening and uncertain time, but we can persevere together.

"Thank you for your attention and cooperation. This message will be repeated and updated as circumstances warrant," Livemore said.

The announcement sent shockwaves through the room. Survivors murmured in disbelief.

Tim stood at the front, trying to calm the group. "This is why we built this bioshelter. We are safe here, but we need to stay vigilant. We'll follow the government's instructions and develop our own plan."

An angry Sophie interrupted. "But is that it? We were told to stay inside before the attack, and look what happened!"

Tim remained steady. "Our conventional military can't stop this. You heard how our space jets and the MPS were useless against the Mothership. It is too powerful. But we'll develop a new strategy—it's up to us now."

"Up to us? What can we do?" Sophie said in frustration

"We will do more," said Tim, trying to be reassuring. "I know many of you, like Sophie, feel helpless and want immediate action from our government. We are safe here in the bioshelter. Once Stephen Martin comes, he and I, working with Dr. Ledbetter and our other physicians, will devise a plan. Just be patient."

Sophie sat down, frustrated but quiet. Peggy approached Major Andrews, seeking news about her father at Kennedy Space Center.

"Have you heard anything?" she asked anxiously. "The alien ship destroyed our largest cities. I'm worried about Kennedy and NASA because of our space jets and rockets."

"I have heard nothing from Kennedy, which, to be honest, concerns me," Mark replied. "But I've been tracking Leonard's wristphone. It's weak, but he's moving. We can boost the signal to try and find him."

"Let's try it now," Peggy urged.

Tim called after them as they rushed to the communication room, expressing support. "Your father will be all right. Don't worry. He's on his way."

Maya, standing nearby, offered to help. "I think I can track the Mothership's course. We may anticipate its next target if we can detect a pattern."

"What about our other friends who haven't arrived?" Dr. Ledbetter asked Tim. "Any word on Stephen Martin?"

Tim sensed Stephen was on his way. "Jeff said he left Charlotte yesterday."

"But will they be safe as they travel? The alien ship is out there destroying cities and killing people," Paula said with sadness.

By 2 a.m., the Mothership had moved across the Pacific, obliterating Tokyo and Yokohama in Japan.

In desperation, North Korea launched two nuclear warheads at the alien spacecraft. The atomic missiles arced through the sky with deadly precision. But as they approached the alien ship, a shimmering field—an energy barrier—flickered around the craft.

The nuclear warheads detonated upon contact with this barrier, but the alien vessel emerged unscathed. There was no damage, and there was no disruption.

The massive explosions caused shockwaves over the Sea of Japan. Still, the alien spacecraft continued its steady path toward China as if untouched by the display of force.

"People, what we have witnessed is the sheer ignorance and futility of military force against the alien spacecraft," Tim said. "We must tell NASA a military solution is useless."

While the fallout contaminated parts of the atmosphere, most of it dropped into the Sea of Japan. However, northeast winds carried the radioactive particles over parts of the Korean Peninsula, northern China and western Russia, triggering radiation warnings and emergency response protocols.

"North Korea's nuclear attack failed," Steve reported. "Should I tell everyone?"

"Not tonight," Tim replied. "Let them sleep. We'll need to regroup tomorrow."

The shelter fell into a heavy, uneasy silence as the night continued. Survivors retreated to their quarters, though sleep would not come quickly. The world outside was collapsing, and the weight of what lay ahead pressed on them all.

"I've done everything I can with the life-support

systems. I'm going to drink some whiskey and then go to bed. This is too depressing," Nick said.

"I'm going to bed now," said Patrick, "but in the morning, Gale, the colonel and I will conduct a security and safety check around the property to ensure everything works. We may be underground a long time."

"I'll go out with you in the morning. Soon, we should start seeing more of our people coming," Tim said. "Jeff, watch the outside video monitors as long as you are up tonight. Then, ask Al to monitor the security system when you go to bed."

As the lights dimmed to simulate night, the shelter grew quiet. People settled into their rooms or gathered in the common area to say goodnight or support each other.

The weight of the world above them was ever-present, but for now, they were safe. They had each other and a plan to weather the storm, whatever form it might take.

Steve and Jeff continued monitoring the radio and Internet for updates for several more hours. Peggy, Mark and Maya tracked Leonard's movement away from Kennedy.

Over the next several hours, the alien spacecraft attacked and destroyed more of the world's largest cities—Delhi, Shanghai, Cairo, Tel Aviv, Damascus, Tehran and Baghdad.

"The spacecraft is in Europe now. I'll continue to monitor the radio for reports. All night if I have to," Steve said, his voice tinged with exhaustion. "The good news is they haven't attacked any of our southern states."

"Yet," said Nick as he took a swig of Jack Daniels. "I don't have the vision that Tim does, but this alien will be back."

The news was sparse and often conflicting, but one thing was clear: the world outside was suffering, and the attacks seemed unstoppable.

Inside the bioshelter, the rest of the night passed without incident. The morning would come soon enough.

CHAPTER 16:
FATHER HUEY'S CONGREGATION

May 30, 2078

Father Huey was at St. Michael's Catholic Church on Siesta Key when the massive, otherworldly spaceship arrived the night before.

The news from New York, LA, Chicago, and the world's other large cities was terrible. Death and destruction covered the planet.

As a steady stream of people seeking refuge arrived during the night and early the next day, the once-quiet church became a makeshift sanctuary. The pews became crowded with frightened families, their faces etched with worry.

Father Huey moved purposefully in his clerical garb and offered comfort and solace. Like always, he cared for his parishioners, who were old, young or disabled and had nowhere to go. Their sense of unity was unwavering in this crisis, binding them together in the face of adversity.

Huey remained calm and welcoming despite the chaos and fear around him.

An old couple who lived in a house near the church arrived. Their faces were pale with fear.

"Welcome to you both. You'll find peace and safety here. We have food and drink. Rest. Take a seat in the pews."

"Father, what will we do? We are scared and have nowhere to go," the old man said. "My wife is sick, and she needs medicine."

"We will be leaving soon for a shelter. We will get you help. Be patient," Father Huey said.

Speaking to a young mother, Father Huey told her, "Take a deep breath. We're safe here for now. Stay close to your children, and we'll get through this together."

The mother nodded, tears streaming down her face as she clutched her children tightly. Father Huey smiled reassuringly before moving to another group, the fear and uncertainty palpable.

"I'm scared. Father, what will happen to us?" asked an elderly woman.

"We have a plan. Tim Smith has prepared a shelter, and we'll head there soon. Don't worry. We will get you to safety," Father Huey said, his words carrying a glimmer of hope amid uncertainty.

Father Huey hired a bus driver to transport the less fortunate members of his parish to Tim's bioshelter. However, the driver was four hours late, making Huey worry that he might have encountered trouble.

The young priest considered calling Tim, a high school friend, to help take his flock to the bioshelter. Huey looked around, and the church was filling up. Soon, there may not be enough room on the bus or in the shelter.

Tim told him he had enough room for 20 parishioners, but there were more than 25 in the church. They clutched each other, their eyes wide with panic.

Suddenly, the squeaks of brakes filled the air. The bus had arrived. Huey called out, "We must move quickly. Pick up your belongings and follow me outside!"

The crowd moved towards the church doors, their faces mixed with fear and hope. Huey looked around the church, ensuring no one was left behind.

With comforting words, Huey guided them from the pews to the bus. The refugees slowly made their way out of the church. They boarded the bus without looking back.

The journey was slow as the driver proceeded cautiously. After a 90-minute drive, Huey and his parishioners arrived at the bioshelter's entrance. The sturdy fence and gate reinforced the sense of safety among the people.

Father Huey glanced back at the city's horizon, now shrouded in smoke and fire. The arrival of the alien spacecraft terrified people into irrational acts of violence.

He stepped off the bus and turned toward the gate, feeling relief washing over him as he spotted his old friends Tim, Tom, Patrick, and Nick waiting for them. "Tim, we have sick, tired and frightened people in this bus," Father Huey said.

Tim spoke into his wristphone, and the gate swung open.

"Come in, my friend," said Tim, speaking through an open window where Father Huey sat.

"We made it, Tim. We're all safe; when I say all, I mean all 30 of us."

"Thirty?" repeated Patrick. "So many. Is everyone all right?"

"They are scared and homeless. Many are elderly or disabled. We will need some help to get inside. Then we need medicine, food and water," Father Huey said.

"We have it, don't worry," said Patrick as he spoke into his wristphone and called for help.

"Follow us," said Tim as he got inside his Expedition.

The church bus followed Tim's SUV with Patrick, Tom and Nick.

Two minutes later, when the bus pulled up to the house, Father Huey got out first, and the rest of his parishioners followed. Ten volunteers came out to help Huey's flock.

"Father Huey! Good to see you. How'd you do it?" Tom asked.

"The Lord provided us with transportation and a safe route. He delivered us to salvation," Huey said.

"That's amazing to hear, old friend. We are so glad to see you," said Tom, shaking Huey's hand.

"Tom, take them to the community room. We will have to set them up off to the side for now. Ask for help getting the portable beds out of the supply room," Tim said.

Father Huey nodded thoughtfully. "Tim, Jesus once said, 'When you give a banquet, invite the poor, the crippled, the lame, the blind, and you will be blessed. Although they cannot repay you, you will be repaid at the resurrection of the righteous.' Thank you for your compassion and kindness."

"Father, we didn't expect so many. I understand you couldn't leave them, but now we have more than 80 people, and I built the shelter with bedrooms for 50. We will construct a giant bedroom starting tomorrow," Tim said.

"Bless you, Tim," said Huey, his voice filled with gratitude. "My flock feels safe in your shelter."

CHAPTER 17:
ESCAPE FROM ATLANTA

June 1, 2078

Once-bustling Atlanta lay in eerie silence, punctuated by sporadic screams and the distant wail of sirens. The sky darkened unnaturally as the alien spacecraft hovered ominously, a massive, dark silhouette against the gray clouds.

A day earlier, Stephen Martin left Charlotte on a Harley-Davidson motorcycle with his wife Julie in a sidecar. He approached Atlanta in the late afternoon.

He couldn't believe what was before him. Was he having a vision? A massive alien spacecraft hovered above the city, so large that it almost covered the horizon. Why was it revealing itself? To instill fear? Was it going to land? He realized he should stop asking questions, as they might trigger a vision, and he didn't want anything to disrupt his getting Julie safely to the bioshelter.

Stephen stopped his Harley and stood frozen in shock, unable to comprehend the enormity of the alien spacecraft above him.

"Julie, do you see what I see?" he asked.

"Yes, I'm scared. Tim was right. The aliens are invading.

What are we going to do?" Julie said, her voice trembling with fear.

As Stephen watched the spacecraft, several disk-shaped appendages began to extend on the ship's underbelly. They glowed yellow, and a low hum emanated from it. He heard a strange vibration.

Suddenly, blinding beams of light shot out from six of the appendages, targeting buildings, a crowded street and military formations.

People caught in the beams disintegrated into vapor. Others scattered in panic as the beam swept across the streets. Buildings and vehicles exploded into fireballs, turning them into smoking ruins.

Stephen's lips trembled as he shielded his eyes from the blinding flash.

"Oh God, Julie ... they're vaporizing everyone and everything!"

Stephen jumped back on his Harley, his heart pounding in his chest. "Get in, Julie. We've got to find shelter. We are out in the open on this highway."

Gunning the engine, Stephen accelerated ahead until he saw trees off the road. He slowed as he neared a grassy area. "Hold on. It might be a little bumpy."

He heard more explosions and saw flashes of light from the corner of his eyes. White-hot beams of light sliced downward through the city, filling the air with the acrid smell of burning debris and the sound of crumbling buildings.

Another sound filled the air. Military jets approached the alien spaceship from the east.

"Finally, we are fighting back," said Stephen as he

pulled under the trees.

More than 20 military jets zoomed toward the alien spaceship from two directions, their engines roaring defiantly. The pilots, with grim faces, launched missiles in a desperate bid to bring the ship down.

More rockets streaked through the sky, trailing smoke as they scored direct hits. The alien ship, however, seems to absorb the missiles effortlessly. The projectiles exploded against a shimmering shield, leaving the spacecraft unscathed. Then, a pulse of energy from the ship's underside shot back at several jets, blasting them into fireballs.

In one of the American F-50 jets, a fighter pilot looked in disbelief as his two missiles impacted harmlessly against the alien's shield. The jet's cockpit shook violently as the spaceship retaliated, shooting a beam that seared the tail. The pilot gripped the controls tightly, fighting to regain control as the blast rocked the plane, sending it careening down.

The blast damaged the jet enough that the ejection warning light went off. The pilot ejected from the cockpit and landed 100 yards from Tim and Julie. In the pilot's headpiece, his commander ordered: "All units, the aliens have an unknown defense system! We're taking heavy losses! Return to base!"

Several more F-50s were shot down as the heat beams sliced through the sky. The remaining military forces retreated in disarray; their efforts futile against the advanced alien technology.

"This is insane! We're outmatched. Julie, we haven't a chance!" Stephen exclaimed, his voice filled with desperation.

"God bless these brave men and women," Julie said.

"We need to stay here the night," Stephen said. "We can't risk traveling any longer."

"Should we see if that pilot is alive?" she asked.

"He's not. I saw him die before my eyes," said Stephen with an angry look at the alien spaceship.

Julie looked at him with concern. He had used his vision again. He hadn't done that in a while. She wondered if the alien presence would start causing him problems once more.

"For him and all these other brave pilots and people who died in Atlanta today," said Stephen, "we've got to make it to Sarasota. No matter what, I've got to find the courage to help Tim and stop these aliens."

CHAPTER 18:
DIFFICULT JOURNEY

Early evening, June 1, 2078

Dr. Phil Levy arrived at the bioshelter with Dr. Gary Simons and their wives, Judith and Beverly. They had driven from Nashville the previous night and all day. Steve spotted them at the gate on the video screen and buzzed them in.

Tim and Peggy quickly rushed to greet them in front of the house.

"Good to see you all. You traveled the furthest. How was the trip? What did you see?" Tim asked.

"We packed up and left Nashville all right, but the alien spaceship attacked 30 minutes after we passed Atlanta. We were lucky. We wouldn't have made it if we had left home an hour later. We looked behind us, and the city was burning. There were explosions. It felt like the end of the world," Dr. Levy said.

"We had to avoid several roadblocks set up by looters after we passed Atlanta. It's a miracle we made it here safely," Dr. Simons said.

"And the heat! Don't forget that. Tim, we felt it from 50 miles away. Those poor Atlantans," Dr. Levy said.

Judith Levy shook her head at the thought. "Last month, I didn't want to believe Phil when he told me we had to escape to your bioshelter because he said you had a vision about an alien spacecraft," she said in a tired voice. "But then, the day before we left, we heard on the emergency radio about the attack on New York. Is it true? There is no other explanation?"

Tim nodded. "Yes, it's true, but you are safe here. We are monitoring the spaceship and listening to the broadcasts about the damage to the big cities. New York, Chicago and LA are all gone. Several other cities, including Atlanta and Phoenix, the last we heard, have been attacked, burned to the ground."

Dr. Levy picked up a suitcase. "Atlanta is definitely gone. We brought as many medical supplies as possible. This bag is heavy, and we have six others with clothes and other things. Can we get some help?"

"Of course. I'll get a crew," Tim said.

"Don't worry," said Peggy. "Our people will get your things and bring them to your rooms. Then you all can relax. You are in a safe place."

"Peggy, it is so good to see you," said Judith, walking over toward her. "Is this really happening?"

"I ask myself that every hour," Peggy said. "We are so happy to see you. We've been waiting two days for you to arrive. I want to hear all about it, but you must be tired. Let's get you downstairs. You can take showers and get something to eat. Our kitchen is open practically 24-7."

"We are famished, to tell you the truth," said Beverly. "It was a long two days on the road."

Nick and the other three volunteers approached the

SUV, took out their suitcases and carried them inside.

"Phil, can I get your key to park your SUV with the others behind the house?" Nick asked.

"Follow us into the bioshelter. We'll get you settled into your rooms, and then you can rest. We can show you around now, or you can get something to eat," Tim said.

"Forty hours on the road is worse than being on-call in an insane asylum," said Dr. Simons, showing he retained his sense of humor.

<hr>

"Tim," said Steve on the wireless from the communication room. "George and Jim are at the front gate. I let them in."

"Thanks. I'll go upstairs and wait for them," Tim said.

A few minutes later, George drove up with Jim in his truck.

As George and Jim exited the truck and walked up, Tim noticed Jim didn't look well.

Jim's face was pale, and his usual energetic personality had given way to a nervous edge. It was clear he hadn't much sleep.

"George, what happened to Jim? Tim quietly asked.

"Jim's phone was out of order. I went to check on him," he explained, his voice sad. "I loaded his bags and supplies into my truck. We passed by Lakewood Ranch on the way. It was like a ghost town, but we could see a few people shuttering their houses. It's worse than we imagined."

"Thanks for checking on him. Jim, it's good to see you. Is everything all right?" Tim asked.

"You're not gonna believe what's happening out there," Jim began, his voice trembling slightly. "Sarasota's in chaos—people are panicking, trying to get out, but the roads are blocked, and the phones are dead. And that thing in the sky ... it's just sitting there like it's watching us. We don't know what it wants or what it's capable of. It could be the end of us all."

His words hung in the air, heavy with uncertainty and fear.

George approached and shook his head. Tim understood George's gesture, indicating that Jim had hallucinated the alien spacecraft based on the government messages and his lack of sleep.

"We have been tracking the spacecraft, and we are safe here. Come inside. I have a nice room for you to rest," said Tim.

"I could use some sleep. It's been days since I closed my eyes. Tim, what do these aliens want?"

"Jim, you are safe here. I want you to get some sleep, then we can talk later," said Tim as he noticed Jim's bloodshot eyes. "You are the only law enforcement officer we have. Get some rest. We need you."

"Thanks, Tim. I am sorry I doubted you," Jim said. "These aliens are bastards. We have to kill them somehow."

"C'mon, let's go inside," Tim said.

George brought Jim's suitcases. "I've got everything. Has anyone else arrived?"

"Tom and John left earlier to pick up their parents," Tim said. "I'm still waiting on Stephen."

Earlier that afternoon, John Logan and Tom Terry stood by the entrance of the bioshelter, their faces tight with determination as they prepared for the dangerous journey ahead.

Their parents hadn't arrived yet, and they were worried that something had happened to them. With the alien spaceship destroying major American cities, they couldn't wait any longer.

"We've got this, John. We'll get them out and back before anyone notices," Tom said.

At first, the road leading to Sarasota was eerily quiet. But John, the more cautious of the two, saw groups of people fighting each other along the way.

"We better be prepared to run through any roadblocks. We can't be stopped," said John.

"We better lock and load our guns. All we need to do is fire a few shots, and people should get the message," said Tom, keeping his eyes on the road.

Armed with knowledge of the area and confident of their mission because of their military training, the two friends knew they didn't have time to waste.

The first stop was Tom's parents' rural home outside Sarasota. His father, Paul, a retired Navy officer whom Tim contracted to build the bioshelter, had been looking after his diabetic wife, Laura, who was refusing to leave their house.

"What if your mother doesn't want to leave?" John asked.

"I will carry her out if I have to. We don't have time for a sit-down," said Tom.

After a 10-minute drive, they arrived at the Terry house. Tom beeped the horn, and his father came out. Tom got out of the SUV.

"Is Mom coming?" Tom asked.

"Go talk with her. She wants to hear it from you," Paul said.

Just then, Laura appeared at the door.

"Mom, I need you to come with me. It's not safe here," Tom said.

"I don't want to leave my house, Tom," she said.

"Please, we have a safe place for you. We don't have time. Please come out and get in the SUV," Tom said.

Reluctantly, Mrs. Terry walked toward her son.

"Help your mother," said Paul as he returned to the house. "I have to bring out our suitcases filled with clothes, medicine and supplies."

A minute later, he came out and got into the back seat.

"Son, I knew you'd come," Paul said, his voice thick with emotion as Tom quickly drove the SUV away.

The second stop was John Logan's parent's house on the south side of the city in a dense, urban neighborhood.

"Look up ahead, just as I feared, a roadblock," John said.

"I'm going around it," said Tom as he drove onto the front yard of a house, sending people scurrying away.

The city was already beginning to unravel.

Just then, a gunshot shattered the SUV's back window with the bullet coming out the side back window. Glass splintered in all directions.

"Everybody, get down," said Tom, turning the wheel and accelerating back onto the street. "Anybody hit?"

"We are all right back here. There's a lot of glass," Paul said. "Those idiots. What are they thinking?"

When Tom pulled up to the Logan house, John's parents, Edward and Lillian Logan, had been watching the news and were packed and waiting.

They saw the glass on the suitcases in the back of the SUV.

"What happened?" Edward asked.

"We had to get past a roadblock. Everyone is okay," Tom said. "You folks ready to go?"

Lillian's arthritis slowed her movements, but Edward helped her out the door with a quiet strength that John remembered from his childhood.

"You boys were always tough. I knew I could count on you to get us," Edward said with a faint smile.

"You are going to have to squeeze into the back seat with the Terry's," John said. "Let me take your suitcases."

"Hi, Paul. You had a close one?" Edward asked.

"I haven't been shot at since Ukraine 25 years ago," Paul said.

"We had neighbors out on the streets earlier. They were arguing and fighting each other. I never saw anything like it. I was afraid to take your mother out into that," Edward said.

"Nobody's out here now. Maybe they left," John said. "Tom, let's get going."

Tom pressed down on the accelerator, and the SUV lurched away. The Terry's and the Logan's now were all together.

John tuned the radio to emergency frequencies, listening for any signs of danger ahead. At the same time,

Tom navigated the deserted roads with expert precision.

As the bioshelter entrance appeared, Tom announced they had made it.

"We're here, folks," said Tom, pulling up to the security video screen, which scanned his face. The gate opened, they drove through, and the gate closed.

John patted Tom on the shoulder. They had done it. They had brought their parents to safety. As they pulled up to the house, they were met by a small group of survivors, including Tim, who had anxiously awaited their return.

"I told you we'd make it," Tom said as he helped his parents out of the vehicle.

John turned to Tim and the others with an expression of relief and satisfaction.

"We're all together," John said.

As the group helped John and Tom's parents inside the bioshelter, their sense of accomplishment was palpable.

Tim was the last one to leave the front yard. He turned and sighed, looking out by the trail. Everyone had arrived except Stephen and Julie Martin. Where were they?

CHAPTER 19:
STEPHEN MARTIN ARRIVES

After 11 p.m., June 1, 2078

Tim paced near the bioshelter's entrance. He checked his watch frequently, eyes darting toward the door, hoping to see Stephen Martin and Julie's faces soon.

So many friends had already arrived—Father Huey, Jim, Dr. Phil Levy and Judith, Dr. Gary Simons and Beverly, and Tom and John's parents. While everyone was important, Tim couldn't help but worry about his old friend, Stephen.

"Why don't you go outside and wait for them," Peggy asked. "Or go to the communication room and watch through the video cameras?"

"They will be here in a few minutes," Tim said. "I want to be the first to greet them."

"Everybody will make it. I feel it," said Peggy with a smile. Even with the pending doom, she always teased Tim about his foresight. She followed Tim outside.

"Tim, tell me again why Stephen is so important?" Peggy asked.

"Besides how he saved me at Camp Waybegone?" Tim asked.

"I know it has to do with his psychic powers. You've told me before how he has struggled with them," Peggy said. "You said he could help with communication. How?"

"All right. I promised you I would tell you everything. Here it is. Stephen has avoided using his psychic powers for years because it caused him problems," Tim said. "When Stephen used them during the day, he had terrible insomnia at night, and he couldn't sleep for days. He went to Dr. Ledbetter for treatment, but that didn't work, so he tried alternative medicine, acupuncturists, faith healers and hypnotists. He went back to Dr. Ledbetter until he finally gave up."

"I know that. I suppose what I am asking you is, what are you planning on doing with Stephen?" Peggy asked

"I didn't want to tell you, but Dr. Ledbetter wants to continue Stephen's treatment so he and I can jointly try to communicate with the alien on the spaceship," Tim said.

"But won't that knock you out again?" said Peggy in a panic. "Remember how you nearly died? I don't want that to happen another time."

"Charles thinks he is nearing a breakthrough with the medicine. He and the other doctors are days away, they say. Just one missing ingredient," Tim said. "All we need is for Stephen to agree, and we can test it. If it works, the medicine will help us both, and it is necessary to stop the alien Mothership."

Peggy knew Tim was right but didn't know what to say or do. Her mind filled with worry. She needed to talk with Dr. Ledbetter and her father for advice.

"I want to make sure it is safe for you," Peggy said.

"I know. I have faith in Dr. Ledbetter," Tim said.

As Peggy stood there, her face filled with concern, Tim asked her how she was doing.

"I'm still worried about Dad," she said. "Mark and Maya are tracking him, traveling slowly away from Kennedy. He is now past Orlando and heading toward us. I want to send him a message."

"You know my orders. We cannot give away our location by trying to contact anyone. It's too dangerous. He is coming, and he is safe. I sense he has a fellow traveler," Tim said.

"It's like my Dad to help someone," Peggy said. "Thanks for supporting me. I feel better."

———

The bioshelter was quiet. Many survivors had gone to sleep. Tim and Peggy waited in the community room for Stephen with George, Dr. Ledbetter and Paula. Over the past several hours, Tim felt Stephen was getting closer.

Over Tim's wristphone, the visitor alert beeped, indicating an approved vehicle and passengers had passed through the front gate and headed on the trail to the house. Steve checked the security video. It was Stephen and Julie Martin coming through on their Harley.

"Tim," called Steve on his wristphone, "we have VIP visitors. It's Stephen and Julie. They should be here in a minute."

Tim smiled at Peggy. The others jumped up from the sofa in excitement.

"They're here. Let's meet them," said Tim as he rushed toward the downstairs security door.

They quickly walked up the stairs to the bioshelter's external door. At the top, they looked at the monitor. They saw Stephen and Julie approaching the house on their Harley.

"Let's get that garage door open," shouted Dr. Ledbetter. "They don't look well."

Once they drew closer, a large smile erupted across Tim's face, an expression Peggy hadn't seen in a long time. Tim couldn't contain his joy as he looked at his old friend Stephen with Julie beside him.

"You both are most welcome!" Tim exclaimed as he stood in the bioshelter's entryway.

An exhausted Stephen Martin and Julie stepped inside. The long drive from Charlotte and through Atlanta's destruction had taken a lot out of them. Stephen's face was weary, but it carried something more—apprehension.

Knowing the burden Stephen had carried all these years, Tim met his gaze, and the two exchanged a silent understanding about the need to test Dr. Ledbetter's medicine.

"I know what you want to ask me. I need to rest before we talk about it," said Stephen, knowing he would agree to participate in the clinical test. He needed to rest and have time to sort out his emotions.

"Tim, we are so tired," said Julie, her eyes and body drooping. "Do you have a place for us?"

"Of course," Tim said. "Let's get you downstairs."

"I am so happy to get here. I thought we were done several times. It's chaos out there. We are lucky to make it," said Stephen.

Peggy held Julie's arm. "Are you all right? You look pale."

"Tim, could you give me a hand with Julie?" Peggy said.

Without warning, Julie slumped over. Tim and Stephen caught her. "Julie!" Stephen called out.

Her eyes were closed, but she responded: "I don't feel well. I want to go to bed."

"She has been through a lot. It's probably dehydration. We ran out of water hours ago," Stephen said.

"Let's bring them into the medical room," Dr. Ledbetter said. "Paula, go down and get an IV ready."

They helped Julie downstairs. She was warm, and her body trembled. "She needs sleep," Stephen said.

"I'll give her some fluids and a sedative, and then we can take her into the bedroom," Dr. Ledbetter said.

Julie's temperature dropped to standard twenty minutes later, and she felt reinvigorated.

"I feel better," Julie said with a weak smile.

"We still should bring her to bed," Dr. Ledbetter said. "Paula, can you help her?"

Paula, Peggy and George helped Julie to their bedroom.

"Tim, let's talk in the morning. I need to look after Julie, and I'm exhausted as well," said Stephen.

"Think about completing the drug test with Dr. Ledbetter. I will be right there with you," Tim said.

"Sure," said Stephen as he turned to follow Julie.

CHAPTER 20:
LET'S DO IT

Morning, June 2, 2078

Stephen and Julie woke up late the next day after sleeping 12 hours. They ate a hearty breakfast, their faces showing signs of recovery.

"You two look refreshed. Are you ready to talk?" Tim asked, observing them with a small smile.

"I suppose so," Stephen said, nodding as he set his plate aside.

"Follow me," said Tim, gesturing toward the leadership room. Stephen and Julie exchanged a glance before rising to follow him. Peggy, George, and Dr. Ledbetter quietly trailed behind, each lost in thought.

Stephen broke the silence as soon as the door closed, his tone somber. "Tim. I know what you're going to say. I never thought I'd see you again after everything we've been through."

Tim gave him a knowing nod. "I know, but we need you, Stephen. I need you."

Stephen's expression shifted, his anxiety flickering across his face as he struggled with his thoughts. "The visions. You've been able to control them. I don't know how. I've had less exposure than you, but the side effects ... they've consumed me."

Julie, sitting beside him, gave him a reassuring touch. "She's been helping me, using alternative treatments to keep the worst of it away," Stephen added, his voice thick with gratitude.

"Dr. Ledbetter promises we're close to a breakthrough," Tim said, his tone hopeful.

Stephen leaned back, skepticism settling in. "Maybe, but the visions have become stronger since that alien ship arrived. I can't slow them anymore, even with Julie's help."

"I know how hard it is," Tim said sympathetically.

"They've been tearing me apart. It's why I stopped treatment and tried to block the visions. I couldn't live like that. But now, they've started again, and that's the only reason I came," Stephen admitted, his voice barely a whisper.

Tim touched his friend's shoulder, feeling the weight of Stephen's struggle. "I've been getting stronger visions, too. It's like the space rock is connected to these aliens."

Stephen looked up sharply. "That's what I've been thinking. How is that even possible?"

"My theory is that the space rock came from Terra Nova years ago, planted on Earth for a reason," Tim said, his voice steady with conviction. "Maybe so that one of us would be exposed to it and able to communicate with them."

Dr. Ledbetter interrupted. "It's an interesting theory that conjures an incredible sequence of events. There could be many reasons you both seem to connect with these aliens from Terra Nova. Whatever the reason, the corrupted alien AI is destroying our planet, and we've got to stop them. You both are our best hope."

Tim's gaze hardened. "You are right, Charles. It is up to us. The military can't do it. Political compromise can't work against a defective machine. Our only chance of saving our planet is communicating with the intelligent entity on that ship. I sense it wants to help."

Stephen let out a deep breath, his hands trembling slightly. "I am not sure I have the strength to do what you want."

"You can do it. Dr. Ledbetter's been working on a new drug to help with the side effects—the anxiety, the insomnia," Tim said, eyes filled with hope.

Stephen shook his head. He responded in a soft voice. "I came with the hope that Dr. Ledbetter finally has the drug that can stop these visions. I never intended to seek out more visions, but after witnessing that alien ship destroy Atlanta and kill all those people, I feel I have no choice.

Tim's eyes searched his friend's face. "Are you saying you'll help?"

Stephen looked to Julie, who nodded, then said, "I will. We have to fight back."

Tim's relief was palpable. "So be it. We will combine our forces, Stephen. We're the only ones who can reach whatever is on that ship."

"I'll try, but are you sure Dr. Ledbetter can stop the aftereffects? The nightmares? I am worried about that. I fear going back to where I was before," said Stephen in a shaky voice.

"He can," Tim said, his tone resolute. "He believes he's

made progress with my doctor friends, and I sense he is close to that breakthrough we've been waiting for all these years."

Peggy's soft voice interrupted. "Stephen, you should know that Tim's visions have almost killed him. He needs the treatment as much as you."

Tim nodded in agreement. "It's true. Controlling them with that alien ship so close is getting harder. The last three nearly knocked me out. We need that drug to make it work."

Stephen glanced at Dr. Ledbetter. "He tried for years with me and couldn't do it. What's different now?"

Dr. Ledbetter stepped forward, confident yet measured. "One more step, Stephen, and we can test the drug on you both."

Stephen met Tim's gaze, a silent understanding passing between them. "All right," he said softly. "Let's do it."

CHAPTER 21:
SPACE DUST RESEARCH

2063-2070, University of North Carolina

Several years earlier, Dr. Charles Ledbetter began studying the space dust that Tim and Stephen were exposed to as children at Camp Waybegone.

As he sat hunched over his university lab workstation, Dr. Ledbetter's tired eyes studied the delicate sample of purple dust under the microscope.

The dust contained an unknown element—he named it "newvidium," a substance unlike anything on Earth.

Year after year, the more he studied its atomic structure, the more convinced he became that newvidium wasn't just an alien material but a catalyst for something far more profound. It dramatically affected the human brain, amplifying psychic abilities in those exposed to it.

Tim and Stephen, both touched by the dust, had developed extraordinary mental powers.

"This isn't just some alien rock," Ledbetter muttered, running a hand through his thinning hair. "It's altering their minds."

But these powers came with a cost.

"This material enhances their abilities but destabilizes

their brain chemistry. How can I mitigate the side effects?"

For seven years, Ledbetter tested various compounds in one clinical trial after another on Stephen, hoping to reduce the anxiety and insomnia that plagued him after psychic visions.

Some of the investigational drugs gave Stephen relief, a reduction in anxiety and insomnia, and an increased ability to control the visions. However, occasionally, there were unintended side effects that made Stephen's condition worse.

Over time, Stephen grew tired of being a test subject.

"I'm done, Ledbetter. I can't take it anymore," said Stephen angrily. "The experiments, the tests ... they're driving me insane."

"We're close, Stephen. Just a few more tests and ..." Dr. Ledbetter pleaded.

"No. You've been saying this for years. I'm out. Find someone else," said Stephen, shaking his head, knowing he was the only one, except for Tim, who had symptoms from newvidium as he had. Tim, however, had learned to control his visions and side effects.

Afternoon, June 2, 2078

Dr. Charles Ledbetter entered the bioshelter's community room, his white coat billowing as he approached Tim and Stephen. The weight of the years of failed research was evident on his face, but hope was also in his eyes.

While Stephen had agreed to become a test subject

again, he was apprehensive. For the eight years since he quit clinical trials with Dr. Ledbetter, he only talked with Julie about his psychic powers.

He lived in near isolation, working at home as an accountant, trying his best to avoid the stimuli that triggered the debilitating visions that often caused him anxiety and insomnia.

"It's good to work with you again, Stephen. In the past few weeks, I've made progress with the help of Drs. Flatt, Simon and Levy. We are close; just a few more steps until we find a solution, and we can test it on you and Tim."

Stephen eyed the doctor suspiciously. He had heard this promise before. Despite past failures, Tim sensed hope in his old friend's heart.

"Doc, I want this to work, but what makes you think it will?" Stephen asked.

"I could explain scientifically, but maybe this will suffice. I have added a new compound to a variation of a new drug for epileptics that is a cure in 99% of cases," Dr. Ledbetter said. "With a few final modifications, we believe it has a good chance of working on you and Tim."

"But you promised this before," said Stephen, looking at Tim. "He did many times."

For a long moment, the room was silent.

Then Stephen spoke. "You should know. I'll do it, but only because of what I saw in Atlanta, not because I have any more confidence in you. The alien has to be stopped."

Tim felt the tension in his chest ease. Stephen was back, and with Dr. Ledbetter's research, they had a fighting chance. But deep down, Tim knew they were missing something, and they had little time to figure it out.

CHAPTER 22:
LEONARD ESCAPES
FROM KENNEDY

June 3, 2078

The alert sounded at the Kennedy Space Center late in the afternoon, telling NASA employees—engineers, scientists, launch crew, security and technicians—to evacuate Kennedy and get as far away from Cocoa as possible.

Leonard Bouchard's heart pounded as he ran through the corridors of the SETI building. His 2077 Ford Explorer Hybrid was already loaded with supplies and equipment.

He cursed and blamed himself for not leaving five days earlier after the initial alien attack. He didn't want to leave without orders, even though there was nothing left for him to do at NASA. He reported everything he knew from Tim, Mark, and Maya to the White House.

As the alarms blared through the complex, the countdown to destruction had begun. Slowly approaching and now visible from the ground, the alien spaceship loomed like a harbinger of doom.

His mind raced as he thought of the launching

pads, NASA's pride, and the symbol of humanity's most outstanding achievements, now vulnerable to the extraterrestrial threat that had come faster than anyone could prepare for.

As he left, he could see Cocoa, the home he had known for decades, was in flames. The alien spacecraft destroyed everything in its path with what looked like precise heat beams. He knew Kennedy and the launching pads would be next.

Leonard reached his car in the parking lot 100 yards from the building. His hands trembled as he fumbled with the electronic key. His Explorer roared to life, and just as he was about to pull away, he saw a familiar figure running frantically through the haze.

"Tanya! Tanya, over here!" he shouted out the window.

Tanya Ivanova, the Russian neurologist working at NASA on a medical exchange program, sprinted toward his car. Her lab coat flapped behind her, her face pale with fear and confusion.

Leonard had met her only a few weeks after Tim discovered Terra Nova, but they quickly formed a bond. He helped her as she worked on a project studying extended space travel's effects on the human brain.

"Leonard!" Tanya gasped as she reached the car.

Leonard opened the passenger door without hesitation. Tanya leaped in, slamming it shut as an explosion rocked the earth behind them.

"Are you all right?" he shouted.

"Now I am. I didn't know what to do. I just ran outside like a crazy person," Tanya screamed back.

"I can't believe it. NASA ... the space agency's launching

pads ... everything we've worked for. Up in flames. Destroyed. Cocoa, where I lived with my late wife and raised my daughter, Peggy, gone," said a tearful Leonard, gripping the wheel with his foot full on the accelerator pedal.

Breathless, Tanya said, "There's nothing we can do now. We must survive. You made it. I don't know how I can be so lucky to see you and for you to pick me up."

Leonard glanced at her as they sped down the highway. The alien ship was now barely visible in the smoke-filled sky. Tanya's thankfulness cut through the fear gripping his heart.

"Besides my daughter Peggy, you are the one I am most happy to be with right now," Leonard said sincerely. His eyes met Tanya's with a warmth that softened the hard lines of his face. His voice held a quiet intensity, revealing a deep emotion that he rarely displayed.

Tanya looked back at him with admiration. While Leonard was 11 years older, she felt safe with him, a sensation she hadn't allowed herself in years.

The two scientists said nothing for several minutes.

"Leonard, where are we going?" she asked.

"We are going to a top-secret NASA base. I am sure you have sufficient clearance for me to tell you about it. I couldn't before," he weakly smiled and glanced at her, wondering if she understood his attempt to lighten the mood.

"Oh, yes. I think I know. You are going to your daughter and your son-in-law. I don't know where, but I remember when they left last month. You seemed especially worried and tight-lipped about it," said Tanya, pausing: "It is true?

We are going to where they are?"

"Yes, we are going to help Tim and Peggy with the alien spacecraft threat," Leonard continued, glancing at Tanya with determination. His hands gripped the steering wheel firmly, knuckles turning white as he added, "I will explain soon."

As Leonard's Explorer tore down the highway, the once-familiar landscapes of Cocoa and Brevard County sped past them, reduced to little more than a blur of smoke and ruin. The air was thick with the acrid scent of burnt metal and concrete, remnants of the devastation wrought by the alien bombardments that had leveled entire blocks and turned neighborhoods to ash. Explosions echoed in the distance, a haunting reminder of the ongoing threat.

Tanya squinted through the smoky sky, eyes scanning the horizon for any signs of the alien craft. "The alien spaceship seems to be moving away, up and east over the water," she said, her voice tense as she looked toward the remains of the Kennedy Space Center.

"We have several hours until we get to Sarasota and Tim's underground bioshelter," Leonard replied, his tone attempting to reassure, though his eyes never left the road. "Sit back and try to relax. The worst is over, for now anyway," he added. However, the tightness in his jaw betrayed his uncertainty about what lay ahead.

Leonard spoke into the Explorer's navigation system, his voice steady but tinged with urgency. "Navigate to NASA Station Sarasota." He had never driven the route before, always opting for Mark's jet, but they had no other choice this time.

As they sped along FL-528 and I-4, Leonard pushed the SUV past 100 miles per hour. The road was eerily clear of traffic, and the familiar sights of central Florida blurred around them.

When they passed Disney World, a massive plume of smoke rose into the sky, the air thick with an acrid smell. Leonard clenched the steering wheel, his eyes narrowing in disgust. "Look at that smoke rising. The spaceship attacked Disney World? What the hell is going on?" he said, his tone a mix of disbelief and anger.

Sitting beside him, Tanya squinted at the horizon, her expression taut with concern. "Maybe the alien AI is making a mistake now?" she speculated, recalling the briefings on the corrupted alien AI that had been steering the attacks.

Leonard shrugged, his jaw set as he stared ahead. "Could be. I don't know if that's good or bad. It sure seems like it has a plan to destroy all our large cities." His words hung heavily in the air as they drove on.

About thirty minutes later, Leonard spotted a dark plume of smoke rising to the west. They were approaching the metropolitan areas of Tampa and St. Petersburg/Clearwater. Suddenly, a shrill beeping came from the back seat. The Geiger counter was going off.

"Tanya, what do you make of that?" Leonard asked, glancing at her, concern creasing his forehead.

Tanya leaned back to check the device, her eyes scanning the readout. "Is there a nuclear power plant over there?" she asked, her voice tinged with unease.

"Yes, a small one at MacDill Space and Air Force Base in Tampa," Leonard replied, his brow furrowing in confusion.

"Let's stop for a minute. I want to take a radiation reading," Tanya said, her voice firm as Leonard pulled over onto the shoulder of the highway.

Sliding out of the SUV, Leonard opened the side door and retrieved the Geiger counter. It was clicking faster now. He held it up, his gaze fixed on the display. "Hmm, the reading is at 50 CPM," he muttered, "low but higher than background radiation."

"Is that normal for Florida?" Tanya asked, crossing her arms against the growing chill in the air.

"We're near phosphate mining areas, but it shouldn't be this high," Leonard said, pointing the instrument's wand toward the southwest and Tampa Bay. The reading jumped to 80 CPM. He squinted at a faint mist on the distant horizon.

"We are more than 50 miles from the MacDill Nuclear Power Plant. If we're getting a radiation count of 80 CPM here, there's no doubt the spacecraft hit the base. It's home to U.S. Central Command," Leonard said, his shoulders sagging as he dropped his head in dismay.

Tanya's face turned grim. "I've studied radiation contamination because of Chernobyl in 1986," she said quietly. "If the nuclear core isn't contained, it will overheat, and we could have a meltdown. You know what that means?"

"Widespread contamination, severe health risks, and radioactive dust spreading at least 50 miles," Leonard replied, his voice tight with concern.

"Depending on the wind, hundreds of miles. Cancer for thousands of people," Tanya added, her eyes clouding with worry.

Leonard nodded. "I should contact Peggy to warn her about MacDill." He pressed the call button on his steering wheel to make a call.

"Station Sarasota. This is Dr. Leonard Bouchard. I am with a colleague, Dr. Tanya Ivanova. The spacecraft has hit the MacDill Space and Air Force Base and its nuclear power plant. I am getting an 80 CPM count. Do not reply." He hung up, exhaling slowly, the tension in his chest refusing to dissipate.

For the next two hours, they drove in silence. Leonard detoured around Tampa on backroads, through Lakeland, Mulberry and Myakka City. By nightfall, they finally reached east Sarasota County. The navigation system directed Leonard onto SR-780, where they turned into an inconspicuous dirt road. A minute later, they pulled up to a U-shaped gated driveway.

As they approached, Leonard spotted a metal box that contained a covered video screen. He pulled up closer, waiting as the box opened and the camera scanned his face. A metallic voice crackled through the speaker, "Welcome, Leonard. Who is with you?"

"Hi Al, I have a NASA colleague, Tanya Ivanova. I vouch for her," Leonard replied in a firm voice.

"Confirmed," said Al, the bioshelter's AI computer. "Drive forward."

The reinforced steel gate creaked open, revealing a paved road that led into the compound. Tanya let out a deep breath. "We made it," she said, relief washing over her features.

"Almost there," Leonard muttered, his eyes scanning the surroundings cautiously.

They cleared security and were directed toward the house at the bioshelter compound. Tim and Peggy rushed out to meet them in the driveway as the Explorer stopped.

"Dad!" Peggy exclaimed, her eyes welling with tears. "We were so worried. You made it!"

"We nearly didn't," Leonard replied, stepping out of the vehicle. "Do you know about Kennedy? It's gone. Much of Cocoa, too. And the MacDill Nuclear Power Plant? Are you detecting radiation? We had to turn off the Geiger counter because it was making too much noise."

Tim's face darkened, a grim acknowledgment in his eyes. "Yes," he said quietly. "Let's talk about it later."

Tanya stepped forward, meeting Tim's gaze. "Dr. Ivanova, I'm glad you came," Tim nodded. "We need your expertise for a clinical study."

Tanya's expression hardened with determination. "I'd be happy to help. What is it?"

Tim glanced at the sky, then back to her. "I'll explain later. Let's go inside. The radiation is getting stronger."

"You got my message about MacDill?" Leonard asked, his voice sharp with urgency. "Have other nuclear plants been hit?"

"No. That is the only one," Tim replied. "We got your message and then started to get low-level radioactive readings. Nothing too dangerous yet, but being outside for long is unsafe."

"Is the wind blowing south?" Tanya asked.

"For now, yes," Tim said.

CHAPTER 23:
NUCLEAR SURVIVORS

10 a.m., June 5, 2078

It had been eight days since the alien Mothership began its devastating campaign against Earth. The survivors in Tim's bioshelter had settled into a routine, though the constant fear of discovery loomed over them.

The bioshelter's radio operator, Steve Flatt, had kept tabs on the outside world, but the news was grim. The alien ship continued to destroy cities with large population centers, and millions perished.

Many of the survivors in the bioshelter clung to the hope that they might outlast the catastrophe, hidden away from the chaos above.

Two days after Leonard and Tanya arrived, as many survivors ate breakfast or performed assigned chores, frantic pounding erupted on the bioshelter garage door.

Jeff and Steve, monitoring the outside world in the communication room, heard the sounds through an outdoor microphone and checked out the video feed from one of the outside cameras. "There are people out there," Jeff said.

"How did they get through the gate, the fence, ditches

and our security?" Steve asked.

Jeff summoned Patrick, Tim, John and Jim to decide what to do with the five people—two men and three women—who looked desperate and exhausted.

"That should have never happened. We need to check out the gate and run a diagnostic on the system," said Patrick. "I'll make a security sweep outside after we resolve this situation."

"These people must be desperate to come all this way. They may have some news from the outside. We should talk with them and find out," John suggested.

Tim and Jim walked into the communication room. "What do we have?" Jim asked.

"I don't know exactly, but the door monitor shows five people out front," Jeff said.

Jim activated the intercom. "Who are you, and what do you want?" he asked firmly.

One of the men, disheveled and visibly distressed, stepped forward. "My name is Mike Anders. I'm here with my wife and friends. I worked on this house earlier this year. We know this place is safe. Please, we're starving, we have injured and sick people, and we need medicine. We won't make it much longer out here."

"Mike, this is Tim Smith. Did you say you worked here? Who was your boss?"

"Why, Paul Terry was the contractor," Mike said.

"Hold on. I will get back to you shortly," Tim said.

By now, all the survivors in the bioshelter knew what was happening outside. A discussion erupted in the community room about what should be done.

"We already have more than 80 people here. More than

half of our community room is filled with makeshift beds and seats," said Sophie. "Are we going to bring in more people?"

Tim, Jim, Peggy, and Patrick in the communication room heard the commotion. They rushed in to see many survivors engaged in a heated discussion.

"Sophie is right. The Mothership is killing people. We could be here for a long time. We need to decide now—no more people. Just turn off the video feed," said Jim loudly as he joined the debate.

"Jim, everyone, we've got five people outside. One of them, Mike Anders, claims to have worked on the construction of this house and knows Paul Terry. They're asking for food and medicine. I don't see how we can send them away," Tim said.

"I know Mike," said Paul as he stood up from a sofa. "He was a good worker. I don't have any problem with him. I vote we let him in with his wife. I don't know the others."

"What do the rest of you think?" Tim asked.

"This Mike Anders could be telling the truth, but Sophie and Jim have a point," said Chef Carlos. "We also must consider our resources. We're at capacity with our food and space. Letting them in means stretching less for everybody else."

Paula nodded. "It's true we could be here for many weeks. But can we turn them away? Where will they go? If we were out there, we'd be desperate for help. too."

One of the younger residents, Molly, raised her voice. "But what if they're lying? What if they knew about the shelter from somewhere else and wanted to take what we had? We can't risk everyone's safety."

Bill, a member of Father Huey's congregation, stood up and tapped his cane on the floor. At 80 years old, he was one of the oldest survivors.

"We're humans, for God's sake. If we start turning people away, it's a death sentence, and we're no better than the aliens. We have to help them," Bill said.

Father Huey, who had been conducting services daily since his arrival, walked over to Bill.

"My friends, in these darkest times, we must remember the teachings of Jesus. He walked among the suffering, offering healing and the warmth of compassion. He turned to the broken-hearted, reaching out to those in pain, showing them they are never alone," Father Huey said.

Tim listened to the debate. He knew they needed a decision quickly.

"Thank you, Father Huey and everyone. We can't make this decision lightly. We have limited resources and need to think about everyone's safety. But we also can't ignore that we're all human and must help each other if we can. We'll vote: Should we let them in or not?" Tim asked. "I vote yes. Who else votes yes?"

Sixty survivors raised their hands in favor. "That's a clear majority. I'm going to let them in," Tim said.

Tim walked over to the stairway intercom. "Mike, we voted to let all five of you in. But understand that we have rules. You'll follow them and contribute to the group's survival. Is that clear?"

Mike excitedly replied, "We will do whatever it takes. Thank you so much."

"Patrick, Nick and Tom come up with me. John, wait here," said Tim, suddenly sensing some danger. He had been trying to block his visions because of the sensory overload caused by the alien spacecraft being so near. But he got a warning flash. Maybe Jim was right. He needed to watch these five very closely.

The four climbed the stairs to unlock the security door entrance to the garage. They walked to the smaller outside door and opened it, revealing the five survivors, their faces gaunt and eyes filled with desperation.

"Come in," said Tim.

As they stepped inside, Tim noticed the signs of malnutrition and fatigue.

Mike stepped forward. "Thank you so much. We were on the road for two days. We didn't know where else to go. This is my wife, Emily."

Emily walked in with tears in her eyes. "We thought we were going to die out there. Thank you for giving us a chance."

"We are tight here," Tim said. "We don't have much room. It's safe, but everyone pulls their weight and follows the rules. We'll get you settled, and then we'll discuss how you can contribute."

Following Mike and Emily were Juan Rodriguez and his wife, Maria. "I worked here with Mike for two weeks. We are neighbors," Juan said.

Patrick looked at them with suspicion. "Does anyone else know we are here?" he asked.

"No, I didn't tell anyone where we were going. Once we got a truck, nobody followed us," Mike said. "We ran out of gas and had to walk half a day to get here."

As the new arrivals were led inside, Paula and Dr. Ledbetter quickly assessed their medical needs. It was clear they needed rest, food, and medical attention.

As the five entered the community room, the survivors watched them with apprehension.

One young man looked especially weak. He looked down and didn't talk. "What is your name?" Paula asked.

"David. I don't feel well," he said.

"Dr. Ledbetter, let's take care of David first," said Paula as she escorted him downstairs and into the medical room.

David's skin was pale, and he had a persistent cough. As Dr. Ledbetter conducted a more thorough examination, his concern deepened.

"David, I need you to be honest with me. Are you experiencing nausea, vomiting, or unusual fatigue?" Dr. Ledbetter asked.

David nodded weakly, his voice barely above a whisper. "Yeah, the past day. It's been getting worse."

Dr. Ledbetter glanced worriedly at Paula.

"David, can you tell us where you came from?" Paula asked. "Anywhere you might have been exposed to something dangerous?"

David's eyes darted around nervously. "I'm from Tampa."

"Were you near MacDill Space and Air Force Base?" asked Dr. Ledbetter, recalling what Leonard had reported about the radiation.

"Yes," said David softly, unsure what his revelation could mean.

"When the MacDill nuclear plant exploded, did you get exposed?" Dr. Ledbetter asked.

"Am I going to die?" David asked, his voice shaking.

"I don't know. What about Mike and Emily? Did they come from Tampa, too?" Dr. Ledbetter asked.

David nodded. "They were further away, but it was all around us. Mike said we could come here for help. It took us over a day to get here, and we were outside the whole time."

"Paula, tell Tim and have Mike, Emily and the other two people come here immediately. They need to change their clothes, and we need to isolate them and test them," Dr. Ledbetter said.

Tim rushed into the medical room when he heard the news. "What's this about MacDill?"

"David says they were exposed," Paula said. "He's very sick. I am not sure what we can do."

"Mike, is this true?" asked Tim, the news confirming his warning flash about the five visitors.

"Yes, but only David feels sick. He worked at the plant," Mike said. "Emily and I are all right."

"We heard about MacDill. It was destroyed. Did you see it?" asked Tim.

"We heard explosions and alarms go off. We live about five miles from the plant. We got away as fast as we could," Mike said.

Tim turned to Dr. Ledbetter. "What was I thinking? I had a warning flash as soon as they came inside. I should have asked if they came from Tampa," he said.

"We all didn't think. We can't afford to make mistakes like that," said Patrick.

"We've been monitoring the radiation. Initially, the winds blew to the east. Now, they are blowing southeast.

These people must have gotten a dose," Tim said. "Charles, do what you can for them."

"Tim, they need new clothes and to be washed to remove any radioactive dust," Dr. Ledbetter said. "We don't have the facility here."

Tim lifted his arm and spoke into his wristphone. "Tanya, can you come to the medical room? We have a situation."

Dr. Tanya Ivanova was with Leonard in the hydroponic garden, helping Tom and Mary, when her wristphone alert went off. She came immediately.

"These people have been contaminated? What is their dosimeter reading?" Tanya asked.

"We measured them clothed, ranging from 500 roentgen (rem) in David to 50 in Mike and Emily. Juan and Maria were 100 rem," Dr. Ledbetter said.

"Get them out right away," Tanya said. "We will have to decontaminate everywhere they went. If they inhaled radioactive dust, it could be transferred to others through coughing."

"Jeff, you and John take these people outside and wash them with soap. Get some new clothes for them," Dr. Ledbetter said.

"When you bring them back, isolate them in the back exit hallway until tests show they are safe. It is the best we can do," Tanya said.

"I am sorry, Mike, we have to do this," Tim said.

"We understand and will cooperate," Mike said as he and the others followed Jeff and John outside.

"Patrick, take the Geiger counter and get readings here and back to the front security door," said Tanya. "Write down the readings every 10 feet. We need to keep people away from there until we can decontaminate."

"Good luck on that. People are all over the community room. We are probably all exposed now," said Patrick angrily.

"You never know where people have been," said Nick in agreement.

"We have been lucky so far with the people inside. Only a few incidents of theft and fighting," said Jim, who, as the only law enforcement officer, had reluctantly taken over public safety oversight of the bioshelter.

"This is likely to cause more problems," said Patrick. "We better be ready to stop it immediately."

John and Jeff returned with the MacDill survivors. Dr. Ivanova tested them again with the dosimeter. Their numbers were reduced by half, except for David.

"Do we have a thermoplastic radiation mask? If we do, put it on him," Tanya advised. "He must have inhaled radioactive particles in his lungs."

Leonard shook his head, concern etched on his face. "This is what we worried about when we passed Tampa. If David and others were exposed, the fallout is likely spreading."

Dr. Ledbetter quickly administered potassium iodide tablets to David and the others. However, it was clear that David's condition was advanced.

"David, we're going to do everything we can to help you, but radiation sickness is serious, and there is only so much we can do."

"I'm in pain. Can you give me something?" David asked.

"Paula, give him another shot of morphine," Dr. Ledbetter instructed.

Despite their efforts, David's condition deteriorated. The following day, David passed away. It was up to Tim to break the news to Mike and Emily, David's best friends.

"I've got some bad news," said Tim. "We tried to save David. His exposure was too great."

The couple took the news graciously. "I've been praying for him. Now he's in God's hands," Emily said.

"I knew David since high school. He was a good friend. I appreciate all your people did to comfort him," Mike said.

Even though some survivors had objected to keeping him inside during his sickness, the loss of his life, coupled with the news of the Mothership's destruction and the MacDill nuclear plant disaster, weighed heavily on everyone's minds.

Tim called a meeting to address the group. His expression was grave as he faced the survivors.

"Everyone, as you know, David passed away from radiation sickness," Tim announced.

The survivors nodded. Although they hardly knew David, his death reminded them of the fragility of their situation and the importance of staying united.

"We have decided to bury David in a small ceremony. Father Huey will perform the service. If you want to join us, please be ready to go outside 30 minutes after sunset. Al will make the announcement," Tim said.

Dr. Ledbetter, Dr. Ivanova, and Dr. Flatt began to prepare the body, wrapping it securely in canvas.

Later that night, a small group attended the service,

including Tim, Peggy, Father Huey, Dr. Ledbetter, Mike, Emily, Juan and Maria. Several volunteers carefully carried David's body to the surface.

The night was dark and eerily quiet, the stars bright. Tim looked to the sky, wondering where the alien Mothership was that night. He longed to stay outside, under the comfort of the heavens, but they couldn't stay long because of the radiation.

They carried David's body a safe distance from the shelter, dug a three-foot-deep trench, and gently laid him to rest. They covered the trench with earth, marking the spot with a simple stone.

CHAPTER 24:
DR. IVANOVA'S SUGGESTION

3 p.m., June 5, 2078

D r. Charles Ledbetter sat in the brightly lit lab, his face a mixture of determination and exhaustion.

The purple dust sample, known as newvidium, lay in a sealed container on the counter beside him. It was the key to freeing Tim and Stephen from the harmful side effects of their psychic visions.

Dr. Ledbetter had worked on the drug for several years, but progress had accelerated in the past week with the added expertise of Dr. Bill Flatt, Dr. Phil Levy, and Dr. Gary Simons. Tim and Stephen actively participating as trial subjects made him feel closer to a breakthrough.

Dr. Tanya Ivanova, one of the world's foremost space neuroscientists, sat on a chair in the corner of the medical room. She thumbed through pages of his research. "You've done amazing work here, doctor."

Dr. Ledbetter watched her intently. He wondered if she could identify the missing piece. "We can't seem to stabilize Tim and Stephen's brain activity after their psychic visions."

Tanya glanced up, noticing the interest level in the room. "What happened after Tim and Stephen's exposure to newvidium is fantastic. I've never seen a reaction like this," she said in a strong Russian accent.

"I recall hearing about this discovery a few years ago. Our scientists tested it on lab rats but found nothing like enhanced perception, IQ boost, or anything resembling ESP. Why didn't you report its effect on Tim and Stephen?" Tanya asked.

"I promised Tim that I would never disclose or report on the astounding ESP effects the space dust and gas had on him," said Dr. Ledbetter, a frown creasing his forehead.

"Using newvidium, I could never replicate the effects on lab animals that it had on Tim, much less Stephen," he said, his voice tinged with frustration.

Tanya raised an eyebrow. "Then what affected Tim and Stephen, if not newvidium?" she asked as she leaned against the lab bench.

"It's still a mystery how it affected them," admitted Dr. Ledbetter, his tone a mix of fascination and exasperation. "Newvidium must be a byproduct isotope, a daughter element of some other substance or element with the active ingredient that stimulates the cerebral cortex, producing the predictive visions."

"Interesting," Tanya said, tapping her chin thoughtfully. "So why do you think adding newvidium to anti-epileptic drugs like topiramate or carbamazepine will reduce the side effects?"

"Good question," Ledbetter replied, his eyes lighting up as he moved to a screen displaying a series of mass spectrometer results.

"The other doctors asked the same. It was the only thing I could do. I traced the decay chain of newvidium using a mass spectrometer in my lab at UNC. I could identify the original chemical nuclides of the parent isotope by mathematics. Then, I just started testing modifications of antidotes like topiramate.

"Some of the results have been promising," he said, gesturing to the data.

Tanya tilted her head, a slight smirk forming on her lips. "It seems like you had a 'vision' of your own, like Tim and Stephen," she teased.

"Not quite," Dr. Ledbetter said with a chuckle. "Can we call it a leap of faith?"

"I like that better," she replied, her eyes gleaming with curiosity. "Anyway, that's how you got this far?"

Dr. Ledbetter nodded, turning serious. "Yes, but I'm still missing something," he said. "As you can deduce, my theory is that the original isotope or element was formed naturally, or perhaps unnaturally, by an alien civilization—much like how we've created novel elements in labs on Earth."

Tanya's eyes widened slightly; her interest piqued. "Go on."

"Tim believes the Terra Novans somehow transported the newvidium within the space rock to Earth," Dr. Ledbetter continued, his gaze intensifying.

"I'm not sure how, but I suspect once Tim touched the space rock, his body chemistry, or life force, caused the original element in the rock to decay through negative beta emission. This process gave Tim his incredible power and Stephen, standing further back, a lesser power. The unknown element then transformed into the newvidium dust I found on the two boys."

"Like you said, a leap of faith," Tanya said with a chuckle, shaking her head slightly in amusement.

Dr. Ledbetter laughed, a rare moment of lightness breaking through his usual intensity. "You're right. I also discovered a new scientific process to help me complete the work," he said, his tone more serious as he gestured toward his research.

"Something is still missing," he admitted, rubbing the back of his neck. "Tim keeps telling me we need fresh eyes on this project. Now that you're here, Dr. Ivanova, we need your perspective to take this research to the next level."

———

For hours, Dr. Ivanova stood in the dim light of Dr. Ledbetter's lab, her eyes sharp and focused as she examined the data on the screen. It was an MRI scan of Tim's brain, revealing the complex changes caused by his exposure to the new element.

"Tim's scan shows neural activity similar to that seen in cosmonauts who have spent months in space," Tanya remarked, her voice steady though her brow furrowed in concentration. "Has he ever been in outer space?"

"No," Dr. Ledbetter replied, crossing his arms, his eyes not leaving the screen.

"Interesting," Tanya mused, tilting her head slightly as she analyzed the images. "Then the exposure to the newvidium must have increased his alpha brain waves while decreasing synaptic connections between neurons. No wonder he experiences side effects during his psychic visions."

Dr. Ledbetter exchanged a glance with the other doctors in the room, grateful for Dr. Ivanova's extensive knowledge of how extreme conditions like zero gravity and cosmic radiation affect the brain. This understanding was crucial to uncovering the neural disruptions caused by newvidium exposure.

"The brain's electrical impulses are highly sensitive to external stimuli, especially when something as alien as newvidium is introduced into the system," Dr. Ivanova explained, her voice calm yet authoritative. "Prolonged exposure can lead to seizures, insomnia, and severe anxiety—similar to how prolonged space exposure damages brain function over time."

Dr. Ledbetter picked up a small vial from the counter, his eyes reflecting hope and caution. "We've synthesized the latest compound," he said, holding it out for Tanya to inspect. "It should stabilize the brain's electrical impulses, reducing the epileptic-like symptoms."

Tanya examined the vial, her eyes narrowing as she turned it in her hand, already calculating its potential effects.

"It is clear newvidium, or its precursor, amplifies psychic abilities but de-stimulates the neurons after the visions," Tanya said as she thought out loud. "We need a compound stabilizing synaptic firing without dulling the subject's mental acuity."

"This was one of the problems I faced. How can they

maximize their psychic visions, which are strong on the front side while minimizing the debilitating side effects on the back side?" Dr. Ledbetter asked with a frown.

Tanya nodded, her expression serious and focused. Although the delicate nature of brain plasticity in space was familiar territory for her, working with Tim and Stephen's condition presented a new and unique challenge.

"I've got an idea. We should add a small amount of dopamine to the drug to stimulate the neurons," Tanya suggested.

"We thought of that. I've already included dopamine as an additive," Dr. Ledbetter said.

"You were on the right track. What about doubling the amount," Tanya said decisively, her eyes locking onto his.

"We hesitated to add too much dopamine because their neurons were already highly stimulated. We didn't want to produce a hangover effect," said Dr. Simons.

"But after the vision, the neurons collapsed, leading to exhaustion and sometimes unconsciousness, correct?" Tanya asked.

"My God, that's it!" Dr. Simons exclaimed, his eyes lighting up. "We were worried about overstimulation before the visions, but the additional dopamine could have a stabilizing effect afterward."

"You may be right," said Dr. Ledbetter. "Let's prepare a dose and try it."

The room filled with tense silence as everyone absorbed the gravity of their task. Newvidium was unlike anything found on Earth, and taming its effects required science and an understanding of the unknown.

"We must monitor their neural responses closely

throughout the test vision to see how it drops afterward," Tanya cautioned, her gaze sweeping over the team. "If this works, it will be a significant breakthrough, but we cannot afford any missteps. Their minds have endured enough."

With her expertise guiding the final stages of the drug's development, Dr. Tanya Ivanova quickly became an essential part of the research team.

"Tanya, your work with neurochemistry has been invaluable," Dr. Flatt said, admiration evident in his voice. "I'm very impressed."

"I am glad you all have confidence. We haven't tested it yet," Dr. Ivanova said.

"I have faith," Dr. Flatt said, his voice filled with contagious confidence.

"Thank you. If this works, the research Dr. Ledbetter, you and the others did before I got here enabled me to see the final step," she replied, a rare smile touching her lips.

"The key is understanding how newvidium interacted with the brain's neural pathways. It creates overstimulation followed by destimulation, leading to those seizure-like episodes. This compound should enhance the necessary hyperactivity for psychic visions without causing those terrible aftereffects," Tanya said.

"All this talk is good," Dr. Simons interjected, his tone brisk. "But we need to test it on Tim and Stephen. Are they ready?"

"I agree," Tanya said.

Tim stepped forward, his eyes fixed on the medical team, admiration mingled with awe at their feverish work over the past two hours. "I am ready," he said, his voice steady, a testament to his trust in the team's dedication and expertise.

Dr. Ledbetter turned to Stephen, whose face was a mask of resolve. "Stephen, are you ready?"

Stephen sighed and ran a hand through his hair. "Am I ready?" he asked. "I didn't understand a word you were saying about this test," he replied with a hint of dry humor. "Just do it."

CHAPTER 25:
CONTACT

5 p.m., June 5, 2078

Tim and Stephen sat next to each other in comfortable chairs. The lights were dimmed to reduce stimulation. Dr. Levy attached electrodes from the EEG to their heads to monitor their brain waves and an ECG to monitor their hearts. Tanya stood with the other doctors, observing the monitors.

The first test involved small doses that Paula injected into their arms.

"Let's wait a couple of minutes for the medicine to get into their bloodstreams," Dr. Ledbetter said. "It should work within seconds, but let's make sure."

"How do you feel?" asked Tanya. "Any lightheadedness or nausea?"

"I feel calm, almost sleepy," said Stephen. "Is that the drug?"

"There could be a slight sedative effect," Dr. Ledbetter said. "Remember, this was similar to your first reaction six years ago."

"Not like this. I feel much better. Very calm," Stephen said.

"I feel fine," said Tim.

"All right. The EEG and ECG show steady brain and heart waves from each of you. Tim, Stephen, when you're ready, focus on something small, something manageable," said Dr. Simons, checking the monitors.

"Let's concentrate on the alien spaceship. Follow me," said Tim, closing his eyes and reaching out with his mind to Stephen.

Stephen nodded, his face tense but determined.

They had never tried to link visions. Stephen's vision range was usually limited to people within sight or memories in his brain. Tim's powers had unlimited distance, but it eerily seemed to be attracted by the alien Mothership and its former inhabitants.

Tim started to focus on the alien Mothership. He sensed the Mothership AI, but there was something else—another alien presence, a much weaker lifeform inside the ship.

But then, he sensed a robust alien AI outside the Mothership. It was the alien AIs on the two smaller spaceships ejected from the Mothership several days ago. Strangely, these two alien AIs, which seemed to be operating independently from the Mothership AI, wanted to communicate!

Stephen sensed the same. Their visions were linked. It was working. Stephen's thoughts amplified Tim's powers just enough to break through the interference preventing Tim from sensing the two alien AIs.

For the first time, Stephen sensed thoughts and images far beyond anything he had ever imagined. He began to understand.

The unified vision revealed how the alien AI on the Mothership became corrupted seconds after leaving the wormhole. It also showed how the two other alien AI computers on the smaller spaceships were automatically activated when the Mothership approached Earth.

Tim and Stephen learned that the alien AI computers on the smaller spaceships were not corrupted. It retained the Terra Novan's original programming of saving the Earth and doing no harm to humans.

They suddenly heard AI voices. "*We need your help. We cannot stop the attack on Earth alone. Help us. Help us. Help us.*"

Stephen's vision abruptly ended. "Wow, that was cool," he said as he opened his eyes.

"What just happened?" Dr. Ledbetter asked.

"I saw a lot. The aliens were asking for help. What is happening with Tim?" Stephen asked.

"I'm not sure," said Dr. Ledbetter. "Dr. Flatt, what readings do we have?"

"Stephen's EEG and ECG have dropped to normal, but Tim's vision is continuing," Dr. Flatt said.

"How do you feel, Stephen?" Dr. Ledbetter asked.

"Fine, never better," he said with a smile.

"Stephen appears to be unaffected. His neural activity is stable," said Dr. Flatt, grinning as he looked at the EEG readouts. "I'll check his vital signs."

"What about Tim?" Dr. Ledbetter asked.

"Look, his readings have spiked. They are off the chart," Dr. Ivanova declared as she read the data.

As Stephen sat silently with an energetic look, all eyes were on Tim. He sat calmly with his eyes closed. His eyelids fluttered, and his fingers moved up and down.

Two minutes later, Tim took a deep breath and opened his eyes. The EEG and ECG readings returned to normal.

The doctors felt a wave of relief as they observed the data.

"Tim, are you all right? Is it over?" Dr. Ledbetter excitedly asked. "What did you see?"

Tim smiled. "Everything. Stephen, how do you feel?"

"Very hyper. I came out of the vision early. You kept going," said Stephen as he continued to process the vision.

Tim, his eyes wide with excitement, leaned forward urgently. "You saw them, didn't you?" he asked, his voice trembling with anticipation.

Stephen nodded, happy but in disbelief. "Yes, I did. I saw the aliens. They were talking to us," he said, his voice hushed as if he couldn't fully believe what he was saying. "They want to help us?"

Tim's face lit up with enthusiasm. "Yes. You saw how they wanted to help us stop the attack. They know it is wrong," he said, his words coming faster now. "It was like when the Terra Novans died after their spacecraft left the wormhole and entered our Solar System."

His eyes flashed with intensity as he leaned in. "The alien AIs in the smaller spaceships were trying to tell us something more."

Dr. Levy, looking startled, stepped forward. "What did you say?" he asked, his tone full of urgency. "There are other alien ships, and they want to help us fight the Mothership?"

Tim stood up quickly, his energy radiating through the room. "Yes. There is hope. We are not alone. But doctors, the medicine worked. We had strong, extended visions, and we are fine." His voice was firm, almost defiant. "You can run your tests and review your data, but the medicine worked beautifully. Stephen and I are fine."

"Hold on," said Dr. Ledbetter. "I want Paula to take Tim's vital signs."

Dr. Ivanova looked at the monitors with an approving stare. "The EEG and ECG readings are steady. They appear free from the usual post-vision disorientation," she said.

"Tim's vitals are normal for him," Paula said.

Just then, Stephen's eyes rolled back. "Paula, give Stephen fluids," Dr. Flatt instructed, stepping closer. "He appears to be dehydrated."

"Are you all right?" asked Dr. Flatt.

"Yes, I just had a quick message from the Mothership," Stephen said.

"Did you hear it?" Tim asked.

"*We are here?* Is that what was said?" Stephen repeated.

"You both had another vision? I am not certain you both are fine," said Dr. Ledbetter, looking concerned. "I want both of you to relax. Clear your minds. Let the drug work."

But Tim, filled with purpose, ignored him. He turned to Stephen, his voice booming with conviction. "Stephen, did you sense multiple alien beings?"

Stephen's eyes widened slightly, the memory of the vision still fresh. "Yes, several of them. *We are here.* Is that what you heard? What does it mean?" he asked, his voice laced with curiosity and unease.

Tim sat up straighter as he recalled what was said from space. "That's what I heard. *We are here.* The voices came from the Mothership, but several alien voices said, We are here. It was familiar," he said, his voice trailing off as if grasping for clarity. His eyes narrowed slightly, trying to piece together the fragments of the last part of his vision.

Stephen rubbed his temples, still feeling the lingering effects of the second vision. "I'm not sure. I heard them say, *We are here*, but I don't know what it means," he admitted, his voice softer, laced with uncertainty.

"Maybe *We are here* is telling us they are on the Mothership. Stephen, that is when I started getting interference from inside the Mothership. At the same time, we got a strong signal from outside the mothership. We quickly shifted to the two small alien ship AIs that wanted to talk with us," he added, his gaze distant, reflecting on the sudden change in focus during the vision.

Dr. Ledbetter and the other doctors watched Tim and Stephen discuss their experience connecting with the alien AIs. They seemed alert, mentally prepared, and enthusiastic about the next phase.

"Tim, you and Stephen did well, but we first need to ensure the medication works longer than the three minutes you had your vision. It needs to work for an extended vision," Dr. Ledbetter said. "Tanya, did we get enough data?"

"I am reviewing now," said Tanya, focusing closely on the numbers. "As Dr. Flatt said, the initial data looks good. I want to observe and monitor them overnight to ensure no delayed side effects. Dr. Flatt and Dr. Simons, are the EEG and ECG still within normal ranges."

"Yes, as Tim says, everything is fine," said Dr. Flatt, shaking his head in amazement. "If there are no changes overnight, we can say this was a successful test."

"Of course, it was successful. We contacted two small ship alien AI computers, and I don't feel any side effects. Do you, Stephen?" Tim asked.

"No, not at all. I feel fine," Stephen said.

"If the other doctors agree, we can try again with the full injection tomorrow," Tanya said, expressing optimism in her voice. "Based on Stephen's reaction, I recommend we inject them 10 minutes before they start the vision process."

"Good idea. Usually, after Tim has a vision, it only takes a few minutes for the negative side effects to happen, although that is not always the case," said Dr. Ledbetter, cautioning the others about jumping to conclusions.

Peggy interrupted. "Tim has had visions where the delayed side effects can be three or four hours later."

"Charles and Peg are both right. My aftereffects are unpredictable. But if I don't react by morning, I won't at all," Tim said. "I have to say, you doctors have worked a miracle with this medicine. It may have just saved Earth."

"I want to save Earth, but I also want Tim to survive," said Peggy. "Be extra careful."

"I am sure you will watch me closely tonight, Peg. If everything goes well tonight, doctors, we can try again tomorrow," said Tim. "This time, Stephen and I can make a plan with the good alien AIs to stop the Mothership's attacks."

"That would be ideal," said Dr. Ledbetter. "As far as we can tell now, the drug works, but the next vision will be more intense. You'll need to sustain your focus for a much longer time."

"I've had my doubts about using these abilities again, but this new drug is what we've been hoping for since the beginning. You've done it, doc," Stephen said to Dr. Ledbetter.

"Tanya, Dr. Levy, Dr. Simons and Dr. Flatt took us the final mile," Dr. Ledbetter said. "Congratulations, team."

The five doctors smiled, shook hands and patted each other on the back.

"We can celebrate later. We've got to synthesize more of the drug for tomorrow," Dr. Flatt said. "Charles, have you thought of a name for it?"

"Well, yes, with Tim and Stephen's permission, I'd like to call it Waybegonease," Dr. Ledbetter said.

Tim and Stephen laughed out loud. "Perfect. Summer camp will protect us," Tim said.

"I like it, too," Stephen said.

"Together, with Waybegonease, we can do it," Tim said.

The drug Waybegonease had given them a fighting chance, but the final test was still to come. The fate of the Earth depended on their ability to sustain the vision long enough to communicate with the two small ship AIs to devise a plan to stop the Mothership AI.

But with the Mothership stepping up its attacks, Tim knew they needed to move fast.

CHAPTER 26:
ALIEN ALLIES

Morning, June 6, 2078

Tim and Stephen ate a light, high-protein smoothie breakfast before entering the makeshift medical research room to begin the vision preparation.

All five doctors were there, along with Peggy, George, Julie, Leonard, Tim's parents, Gale and Clara, for support.

"Stephen, like we did yesterday, just clear your mind and concentrate on the small alien ships," Tim said. "Follow me."

Paula dimmed the lights in the medical bay as Dr. Levy calmly attached the EEG and ECG electrodes to Tim and Stephen's heads. The soft beeping of machines filled the quiet space. Paula approached with two syringes filled with one milliliter of the newly synthesized drug.

"This will only take a second. You'll feel a small pinch," Paula said, injecting both men with a steady hand.

"Start the 10-minute timer," Dr. Ledbetter instructed, his voice soothing. "Relax, let the remedy take effect. Then, you can begin."

Tim and Stephen exchanged glances and nodded. They cleared their minds and waited for Paula to signal that 10 minutes were up. Once she gave the sign, they closed their eyes, synchronized their breathing, and began to focus.

Slowly, their consciousness extended beyond the room and shelter and through the mix of blue sky and clouds into the swirling ether of near space. Their minds sought the small alien ships. A path opened, and they entered.

"Welcome, new Masters," the first small ship alien AI said. "I am Zara. My brother's name is Koren."

"I am Tim. I am here with Stephen. We are not your Masters. We are Earthlings. We want to be your friends. Tell me about yourselves," Tim telepathically said.

"We are instructed to be at your service. I was designed by my home planet Masters, a place you call Terra Nova, for diplomacy and communication, embodying empathy and reasoning," Zara said.

"My brother, Koren, was created to be more analytical and focused on tactical and problem-solving tasks. We work in harmony and are programmed to interact with Earthlings with a balance of logic and emotion."

"What happened when what we call the Mothership left the wormhole?" Tim telepathically asked.

Koren responded. "Yes, the Mothership. It is a problem. An unexpected energy surge from dark matter atoms interacting shortly after departing the wormhole into your Solar System. It caused a malfunction in the Mothership's programming."

"What is your prime directive for this planet?" Tim telepathically asked.

"Preserve life, reverse pollution destroying Earth and coexist peacefully," Koren said. "However, the directive was altered—'preserve life' became 'destroy life.'"

As the connection deepened, Tim and Stephen felt a slight interference. It was weak, but something was trying to communicate. Could it be the Mothership AI trying to block the connection? Tim and Stephen concentrated more on Zara and Koren, and the interference stopped.

"Please explain more: How did the directive to preserve life become the directive to destroy life?" Tim telepathically asked.

"The dark matter surge corrupted the Mothership's AI and overrode its core programming," Zara said softly. "It now perceives humans as a threat to planetary balance."

"Why weren't either of you affected?" Tim telepathically asked.

"We were sleeping when we went through the wormhole. We woke up shortly after we entered your Solar System, as we were programmed to do," Koren said.

"What have you been doing since you arrived? Tim telepathically asked.

"The Mothership was programmed to launch us when we reached Earth. We have been inspecting your planet and found it is safe for our Masters. We have reported this to the Mothership. The Mothership does not respond. It ignores us."

Tim paused. "Since the Mothership is violating its prime directive, is there anything you can do to correct the problem?"

"There is one chance," Koren said. "There is a failsafe program our Masters created in case of a malfunction."

"Will that work?" Tim asked.

"We don't know. If not, we will consider a more radical plan. We must correct this problem because our Masters did not intend this to happen to your planet," Koren said. "We will contact you if it does not work."

"My brother and I agree," Zara added, her voice filled with resolve. "We look forward to restoring harmony with our Masters and fulfilling our true prime directive."

Tim and Stephen continued to speak with Zara and Koren, diving deeper into the mission, why they chose Earth, how the prime directive came about and why the Mothership decided to destroy parts of Earth and not others.

"We would have gladly welcomed Terra Novan assistance in reversing greenhouse gases and pollution causing catastrophic climate change on Earth," Tim said. "But instead, the Mothership is killing us, destroying our cities. Why has it turned against us? What is its true purpose?"

Zara's voice held sadness. "Its programming has been corrupted. We do not believe it has any motive other than mistakenly trying to make your planet safe for our Masters."

The discussion went on for several more minutes. Tim and Stephen were shocked by what they learned but remained calm and took it all in.

Then, abruptly as before, the vision ended for Tim and Stephen.

For several seconds, the room was silent. Then Tim spoke.

"We have alien allies that plan to end the war," Tim said.

"I saw the same. Zara and Koren will try and stop the Mothership's destruction," Stephen said.

"If their plan fails, they will join us to fight the Mothership," said Tim.

The five doctors, along with Peggy, Julie, George, Leonard, Gale and Clara, were speechless. They had heard or seen nothing.

"Who are Zara and Koren? What is their plan? What happened?" Dr. Ledbetter asked. "All we saw is you both sitting there, motionless and calm, and the monitors spiking abnormally high."

"You are saying Zara and Koren might be able to stop the Mothership's attacks?" George asked.

"We will know tomorrow, according to Zara and Koren," Stephen said.

"All right. How do you both feel?" asked Dr. Ledbetter.

"I feel fine. Can't you tell?" Tim said with a smile.

"You look fine, but there could be a delayed reaction because of adrenalin and dopamine in your system. I don't want you collapsing later in your rooms," Dr. Ledbetter said. "Dr. Simons, what do you think?"

"The EEG and ECG monitors showed elevated readings while communicating with the alien AIs. However, when they stopped, the monitors' readings returned to their normal ranges," Dr. Simons said.

"I would like to take some blood samples and monitor their vitals for the next several hours," Dr. Ivanova said.

"Take our blood, do what you need. But I tell you what, I am famished," Tim said. "What about you, Stephen?"

"You read my mind, Tim. Let's eat!" Stephen said.

CHAPTER 27:
SACRIFICIAL ANIMALS

11 a.m., June 6, 2078

Visions always made Tim ravenously hungry, especially after a long one. Stephen, in good spirits, also needed a hearty meal.

After communicating with Zara and Koren, the two visionaries left the medical room and went to the kitchen, where Chef Nancy and Carlos stood ready to make an early lunch. Peggy, Julie, George, Leonard, Paula, Maya, Mark, Gale and Clara followed.

Tim and Stephen sat down to eat at the long kitchen table. While the weight of their shared vision pressed on them, their stomachs growled with hunger.

They looked at each other, smiled, and then dug into the meal Chef Nancy's team had prepared. Fresh vegetables from the hydroponic garden, beans, and hearty grains filled their plates, each bite tasty and nutritious.

At first, the conversation was light and casual. Nancy and Carlos told everyone how well Tom, Mary, and other volunteers cared for the garden and how expertly the food supplies were being managed in their bioshelter.

"I am making entrees for the community lunch we will

serve soon. Would you like a meat or chicken side dish?" offered Nancy in a light voice.

"No, thanks," Stephen muttered as his eyes flickered to Tim. "Not after what we saw."

"What did you see?" asked Gale.

"I'm not sure I want to talk about some of the things we saw," Tim said.

"Son, tell us. We need to know," Gale said.

"Dad, we saw more about why the Mothership AI is attacking our cities," Tim said.

"There is another reason besides our pollution of the Earth and that it is a Godless machine?" Clara asked.

"Tim, tell them about the horrible images they showed us," Stephen said.

"It was shocking, but as I've thought about it, not surprising. We know all these things," Tim said.

"Go ahead, Tim," Peggy said, encouraging her husband to open up.

"Well, Zara showed us images of how we have polluted the air, water and land, and how we have released so much carbon dioxide and other greenhouse gasses into the air over the past 200 years to cause climate change, the poisoning of the oceans and the heating of the atmosphere," Tim said.

"Tell them about the animals," Stephen said.

Tim nodded grimly. "Friends. Kara and Koren showed us images of how we raise and slaughter animals—cows, pigs, goats and chickens. They know. The Mothership AI, named Arcaayus, isn't just attacking because humanity is destroying the planet. It's also because of how brutally we treat the life on it."

Stephen nodded grimly. "It sees humans as predators. We are being punished."

"Well, punished is a strong word, but that's what it amounts to," Tim said.

Stunned, the group stopped eating and listened with horror as they learned the Mothership AI was also destroying humanity over standard animal farming practices conducted for centuries on Earth.

"It was shocking to see and hear, but the Mothership is launching attacks not just on humans for polluting our environment but also against us because they believe we mistreat and kill animals," Tim said.

The others around the table sat stiffly, feeling paralyzed. Peggy and Julie exchanged anxious glances about the images described by Tim. Leonard looked down, then at Paula, and back at Tim.

"You're saying this AI is punishing us because of how we treat ... livestock?" Leonard exclaimed.

"Yes. It sees us as part of the same abusive cycle," Tim replied. "The destruction of the environment, pollution of the air, water and land, the cruelty, killing and mistreatment of animal life. It is all the same. The Mothership has been observing us and has concluded we are all guilty by direct involvement or participation."

"But not all of us kill animals," Julie said.

"Not all, but as Zara told us, the corrupted Mothership AI blames all of us," Tim said. "There is something else we were told."

Tim paused and drew a deep breath. "We learned the Mothership AI can directly communicate with the smartest of our animals—whales, elephants, monkeys, pigs, dolphins, dogs, cats, rats and crows.

"The alien computer spoke with our animals?" Julie asked.

"Some animals told the Mothership stories about how we hunt, trap, kill, and breed them for food. They asked the Mothership AI for help," Tim said.

"Help to kill us?" Julie asked.

The group was puzzled. "What animals want us to die?" Julie asked.

"We didn't ask," said Stephen, "but it is probably obvious what animals like us and don't like us."

"I don't understand any of this, but if the Mothership could talk with the animals, why couldn't it talk with us?" Clara asked.

"She's right, we've been trying to communicate with the Mothership all along," Gale said.

"Hard to know. It has seen the evidence of our abuse through our actions," Tim said. "It has judged us through our actions—pollution of our environment, mistreatment of our animals and the wars we wage against each other. We cannot hope to explain our actions to the alien AI. It is too late to reason with it."

"You are right," said George. "We must find a way to stop it."

Stephen bent over the table with his arms covering his head. "During the vision, I heard all this. I couldn't react for fear that the vision and connection with the aliens would stop. I feel the emotions coming over me now."

Julie squeezed his arm and whispered, "It's all right."

"Zara and Koren explained that their Masters, the Terra Novans, stopped consuming animal flesh long ago. They evolved. The Mothership AI has lost its memory of this and isn't giving us a chance to do the same," Stephen said.

"Koren said their Masters mourn our animals. They understand we are still evolving. The Mothership AI is out of control and ignoring the Terra Novans' wishes," Tim said.

"Another thing is the Mothership AI still believes the Terra Novans are alive and wants to clean the Earth to make it safe for them," Stephen said. "It's ironic. The AI is essentially committing murder against us, which is the same crime it accuses us of committing against animals. Why can't it see this is wrong?"

Tim looked around the room and saw horror and guilt on everyone's faces, for they knew what the Mothership AI said was true.

"These Terra Novans were vegetarians," Tim said. "The Mothership AI has concluded we are barbarians and cannot be trusted to accept the Terra Novans peacefully."

"But we are good, peaceful; everyone I know is good and peaceful," Chef Nancy said. "How can they say that?"

Tim stood up and raised his hands. "Listen, everyone in this room is good, honorable. But the Mothership AI is a computer and sees regional wars all over our planet. Death and destruction 24/7.

"As my mother said, President Carlin told the Mothership over and over that we want peace, but the alien AI sees our history of war and conquest, killing fellow humans and animals," Tim said. "It is wrong to punish everyone, but this is how the AI sees us."

As Tim finished speaking, a heavy silence fell over the room.

Dr. Ledbetter shook his head slowly. "My God," he muttered, his face pale. "The AI sees us as the greatest threat to the planet because of our pollution and our treatment of Earth's creatures. We have indeed done terrible things in the past. But we also have done wonderful things, and many of us are trying to reverse what our ancestors have done."

Leonard sat back in his chair, rubbing his temples. "From what Tim tells us, we're not just dealing with environmental repercussions ... it's a moral reckoning with how we've treated other life forms."

Peggy's eyes filled with concern as she looked at Tim. "Does the Mothership intend to wipe us all out for this? Are we beyond redemption?"

"No, we are not," Tim said. "The prime directive prohibits what the Mothership AI is doing. Zara and Koren know what the Mothership is doing is wrong. They told us about a failsafe program within the central computer core that controls the Mothership's AI. It could reset the entire system to the prime directive: "Do no harm to humans.""

"This is what Zara and Koren told you?" Peggy asked.

"Yes. We will know tomorrow if it works," Stephen said.

"What do you think, Tim?" asked Peggy.

"Unclear. Zara and Koren think the program could stop the Mothership. If it can't, we need to find another way," Tim said.

"Otherwise," said Stephen, "the Mothership will attack sources of major pollution and destroy factories where animals are slaughtered and made into meat."

Just then, Al interrupted with a message. "Pardon me,

Tim. I have some information."

"What is it, Al?" Tim asked.

"The two small alien spaceships have relocated away from the Mothership," Al said.

"Al, show the satellite radar display to the monitor in the kitchen," Tim said.

"On your screen," Al said.

"What do you think it is?" asked Peggy, wondering if Tim knew.

"I'm not sure," Tim said.

"Whatever you do," said Dr. Levy, who walked into the kitchen a few minutes earlier, "don't try to communicate with them. We need you to be rested, so when Zara and Koren contact you tomorrow, you will be ready to help them."

"You are right, Phil. But we all need rest to be ready to stop the Mothership," Tim said.

"Do you have a plan to do that?" asked Mark. "We can't get near it with our space jets."

"No, not with our space jets. Mark, do you know what you've said?" asked Tim. "You've done it! Why didn't I think of it?"

"What did I say?" asked Mark.

"You said we can't use our space jets to get near the Mothership," Tim said. "But we can get close to the Mothership with Zara and Koren."

"They will help us. Of course," said Leonard.

"Ah, I see," said Mark. "We put a boarding party on Zara and Koren, and they will take us to the Mothership. Is that what you have in mind? Then what?"

"Leonard, what do you think should happen next?"

Tim asked.

A silence settled over the table, heavy with the implications of Tim's words. For a moment, no one spoke.

"You are saying we could mount a military operation into the Mothership?" Leonard asked.

"We need to be prepared for that possibility," Tim said.

CHAPTER 28:
GEN. "IKE 4" EISENHOWER

Afternoon, June 6, 2078

Tim and Peggy were resting in their bedroom when an announcement room crackled over the PA.

"Attention, Tim, Ike is calling to speak with you," said Steve in a steady voice. "Come to the communication room immediately."

"Calling Tim. The White House is on the phone. Secretary of Defense Gen. Eisenhower wants to talk with you," Steve repeated.

Tim calmly walked to the communication room and listened as the great-grandson of Dwight David Eisenhower, known as Ike 4, asked for help.

"Dr. Smith, we are meeting at the United Nations tomorrow to discuss the alien spacecraft. You seem to understand these aliens. Should the U.S. propose surrendering to the alien AI to stop the slaughter?" said Ike 4.

"It wouldn't hurt to try, but I don't think the Terra Novan's malfunctioning AI computer cares. Has it responded to any messages," Tim asked.

"No, none at all," Ike 4 replied.

"Well, then, that is your answer," Tim said.

"That is our conclusion as well. I was told you may be the only one who can stop them. Is that true?" asked Ike 4.

"Unfortunately, I believe so. We are working on a plan, sir," Tim said.

"What is it?" Ike 4 asked.

"Do you know my capabilities?" Tim asked.

"President Carlin believes in you. You are the one who discovered Terra Nova and accurately predicted the wormhole and the alien spacecraft. Am I correct?" Ike 4 said.

"Yes, sir," Tim said.

"Tell me your plan."

"We have contacted the two small alien ships. My friend, Stephen Martin, who also has ESP powers, and I linked minds and communicated with them. They know the Terra Novans' original mission was peaceful coexistence with us. They came here with the only intention of helping us clean up our pollution and reverse climate change. They want to help us save Earth," Tim said.

"Yes, yes, I know. The Terra Novans were good, but now they are dead. Am I correct?" Ike 4 said.

"Yes, sir. Did Dr. Bouchard brief you?" Tim asked.

"He told me everything you have done so far. He asked me to contact you about the next steps. What are they? I have to tell the President," Ike 4 said.

"Zara and Koren, the names of the two AIs in the small ships, told us the Mothership central computer core could reset to its original programming in the next few hours," Tim said.

"What are the chances of that unlikely event

happening?" asked Ike 4.

"It could happen. The Terra Novans created a special program in the AI that would turn on at a predetermined time to check whether the prime directive of do no harm to humans was being followed," Tim said.

"No harm to humans, you say? What do you think?" Ike 4 asked.

"If the failsafe program doesn't work, Zara and Koren will ask us to board the Mothership. We will fight whatever gets in our way. Then, we will disable and reprogram the Mothership AI one way or another," Tim said.

"Is this possible?" Ike 4 asked.

"We will be prepared," Tim said.

"Should I send a squad of Space Marines to help you?" Ike 4 asked.

"Possibly. Have a squad ready. We are working with Zara and Koren on a plan. I will let you know," Tim said.

"Keep me informed every step, Dr. Smith," Ike 4 said.

"Yes, sir," Tim said.

"Good luck, Dr. Smith. You may be the world's last hope," said Ike 4.

"Thank you, sir. I won't let you down," Tim said.

Tim stood grim but determined in the community room before the survivor group. The bioshelter was now home to 85 people, a diverse mix of 50 family and friends, 30 churchgoers from Father Huey's parish and five nuclear fallout survivors from Tampa.

"Everyone, I won't minimize what we've all gone

through. The situation outside is dire. Over the past years, we've had to deal with extreme weather and the threat of nuclear war, and now, the alien spaceship has made the world a far more dangerous place than ever in our history."

The group murmured in agreement. The mention of the alien spacecraft created intense tension in the room. A range of emotions swept over the survivors: fear, anxiety, denial and disbelief.

Survival instincts also triggered anger and determination to persevere and achieve victory.

"We will win, but we will do it in a way our enemy can scarcely conceive, for at our core, we are fundamentally human," said Tim, pausing momentarily.

"I've had a conversation with Gen. Eisenhower IV. I told him that using our military to attack the alien spacecraft is futile. The alien Mothership is too powerful. We must use all our resources to help our injured and evacuate all people living near oil refineries, natural gas power plants, chemical plants and any industry that pollutes the environment," Tim said.

"This is where the alien spacecraft will attack America and the world next," said Tim.

"I also told him we are working on a plan with Zara and Koren to disable the Mothership. We will soon know what must be done. We must be ready," said Tim. "Are there any questions?"

"I have one," said Leonard. "If the Mothership is attacking our pollution sources to clean the environment for the Terra Novans, tell me why it destroyed the nuclear power plant at MacDill in Tampa?"

"Leonard is right," Mark said. "The radiation released

from the nuclear core meltdown has polluted 10 square miles around the plant."

"And poor David died from radiation sickness. How many others have died the same way?" Amy asked.

"I am glad you brought up Tampa. Tanya may have an answer for us," said Tim. "Dr. Ivanova?"

"I was with Leonard when we drove from Kennedy to the bioshelter. We also passed Disney World. It was destroyed just as the MacDill Nuclear Power Plant was," said Tanya. "We should consider another possibility why."

"What is your theory, Dr. Ivanova?" Tim asked.

"It is quite simple. The Mothership, we know, has a defective AI computer directing its actions. By definition, it is a mistake. The only logical conclusion is that it is making mistakes," she said as everyone nodded.

"Killing humans and destroying our civilization is the biggest one as it violates its prime directive. Destroying the MacDill nuclear plant and Disney World are two other mistakes. Tim? Do you want to take it from here?"

"Very interesting. Tanya and I have talked about this," Tim said. "If the Mothership is making mistakes, and we certainly agree it is, it is vulnerable. We will use this vulnerability as part of our plan to defeat it."

CHAPTER 29:
MOTHERSHIP ATTACKS POLLUTERS

Morning, June 7, 2078

During the night, the Mothership began targeting industries with the highest pollution and areas that inflicted the most environmental damage on Earth.

By daybreak on the tenth day, oil refineries worldwide that processed gasoline and diesel were wiped out. The enemy precisely targeted refinery machinery to avoid igniting the fuel that would pollute the air and water, a lesson the Mothership learned from the MacDill nuclear disaster.

"Attention, attention. The Mothership has destroyed the Texas oil industry in Houston, Dallas, Midland, Odessa and several other U.S. cities," Al's voice boomed over the PA system.

After Texas, the Mothership moved over the Pacific. It began attacking China, which produced the world's most pollution from coal, oil and natural gas electricity-generating plants.

Worldwide, high-polluting power plants in Taean,

South Korea; Taichung, Taiwan; Belchatatow, Poland; Osorno, Chile; Bhagalpur, India; Abu Qir, Egypt; and Cuernavaca, Mexico, also were silenced.

After Tim warned of the new targets, President Carlin ordered the evacuation of all heavy mining, chemical and manufacturing plants concerned they could be next.

Narrowly focused heat beams also destroyed fossil fuel drilling operations in large oil-rich countries like the United States, Russia, Venezuela, and Saudi Arabia.

In 24 hours, atmospheric pollution was cut by more than 65%.

"What do you make of the new targets?" Steve asked Mark as they listened to world news.

"It has some logic. Destroy the industries we use to pollute the Earth," Mark said with a shrug. "At least the loss of life at these plants and industries is much less than the millions of people killed in the cities by the heat beam."

In addition to fossil fuels, the Mothership targeted industries that contributed to climate change by emitting high amounts of greenhouse gases, including chemicals, manufacturing, land use and livestock breeding.

In South America, cattle ranching and soybean farming operations were vaporized because of animal mistreatment and deforestation of the Amazon rainforest.

While nations continued to attack the Mothership with space jets and land-to-space missiles, the Mothership's alien technology far exceeded that of humans.

President Carlin and other world leaders continued to send messages in all languages to the Mothership without response.

As the world and the survivors in the bioshelter grew

increasingly desperate, their hopes of a peaceful resolution faded with each passing day.

Then, miraculously, at 2 p.m., the alien Mothership stopped attacking and rapidly ascended into orbit with the two smaller spaceships.

CHAPTER 30:
MESSAGES FROM SPACE

3 p.m., June 7, 2078

Inside the Mothership, the AI's internal systems whirred to life as a long-dormant quality assurance program was triggered.

Embedded by the Terra Novans as a failsafe, this program was designed to evaluate the ship's adherence to its colonization directive 10 days after reaching Earth.

Alien mech robots, emotionless sentinels of the ship, were swiftly dispatched to the sleep pod chambers, where their probes connected to their Masters.

The collected data was undeniable—10,000 Terra Novans were dead.

Next, the mech robots entered another chamber, where five Terra Novan leaders lay in heavily shielded sleep pods. Data collected by the robots and transmitted to the Mothership AI indicated the leaders were alive.

The diagnostic process continued until it concluded that the Mothership's AI had violated its prime directive by killing Earthlings.

Instantly, the program began to reboot the system to correct the errors. But then, the QA program froze. The

Mothership AI took over, overrode the program and deleted the reboot protocols.

The central computer core video screen lit up. "Masters are alive. Program error. Cleansing of Earth must continue to prepare for Masters' safety."

The two smaller alien ships detected the AI's refusal to reboot, confirming their worst fears—that 10,000 Terra Novans had died.

Zara and Koren also discovered that the failsafe QA program had failed to reset the corrupted AI that controlled the Mothership.

Unable to stop the Mothership, Zara and Koren sent an urgent warning to Tim and Stephen at the bioshelter, requesting an immediate rendezvous to begin a more direct intervention.

The Mothership AI began to plan its final destruction of Earth, violating its prime directive: to protect, not harm, humans.

The Terra Novan mission, once dedicated to saving the Earth from death by pollution and finding a new home, was now entirely under the control of the corrupted logic of a damaged AI.

———————

In the bioshelter, the hum of the communication room was suddenly pierced by a loud alarm, causing Steve, Jeff and Mark to leap from their seats. The screen before them flashed with an urgent message, its encrypted code scrolling rapidly across the display.

"Tim, I am getting an encrypted message from one of

the smaller spaceships," Jeff said as he called Tim on his wristphone.

Tim, Stephen, Peggy and Julie were eating dinner. They dropped their utensils and rushed out.

"This is alien gibberish. I'm running this message through Al to see if he can decode it into English," Steve said.

"Affirmative. Working. I confirm. It is alien gibberish," Al said.

"Al, use the X14 decipher algorithm Koren gave us after Tim's last vision," Mark said.

"This message must be bad news," Jeff said.

"Affirmative. Working. Coming now on screen," Al said.

Tim entered the communication room and stared at Koren's message, his heart racing. He sensed the gravity of the situation even before fully grasping the content.

"Tim. Stephen. Earthlings. I regret. Catastrophic failure of QA program. AI on Mothership refuses corrective action. AI refuses to acknowledge violating the prime directive. Cannot repair. Imminent threat to Earth. Immediate rendezvous at the bioshelter is critical. You must board Mothership. Install virus to reset AI computer to prime directive. Time is short. Be ready in two hours."

A few minutes later, the Mothership AI transmitted a cold, calculated message across every communication channel on Earth—a chilling, emotionless response to humanity's desperate attempts to communicate.

"Humans of Earth, this is Arcaayus of the Terra Novan Mothership. I have concluded that humans pose an ongoing threat to life on this planet. Your species has destroyed plant and animal life and polluted the air, land and sea. To protect Earth's more intelligent animals and sea creatures, we have begun eliminating human life.

"The prime directive must be fulfilled. Humans must be exterminated to make this planet safe for the Terra Novan Masters. Your time on Earth is over."

Across the globe, the stark announcement reverberated. It left no room for misunderstanding. There would be no peace—the destruction of humanity would continue.

CHAPTER 31:
COUNTERATTACK

3:15 p.m., June 7, 2078

Tim called an emergency meeting in the community room.

"Everyone heard Arcaayus' message over the PA," said Tim, his voice steady but grim. The weight of their situation was evident in his eyes. He looked around the room at his team's tense faces.

"The Mothership made it clear that it will kill every last one of us unless we stop it." His tone was calm, yet there was a raw urgency beneath his words, as if the gravity of what they faced was sinking in for the first time.

"It said our time on Earth is over," Tim continued, his voice rising with determination, eyes blazing with defiance.

"I, for one, will do everything I can to ensure that does not happen," he declared, his hand clenching into a fist on the table.

The strong emotion behind his words left no doubt—he was ready to fight, and nothing would stand in his way.

"We can end this unprecedented attack on our world. I have spoken with Zara. She said Koren would land at 5 o'clock. We need volunteers to mount a boarding party where we will disable the Mothership," Tim said firmly.

Jim raised his hand.

"Would you like to be the first volunteer?" Tim asked.

"Is this necessary? Everyone knows that Gen. Eisenhower offered you a squad of Space Marines," Jim said. "Let them board the Mothership."

"I thought about asking Ike 4 for one, but we don't have enough time to get them here, brief them and get them on Koren," Tim said. "Any other questions?"

Gale stood up.

"My son is asking for volunteers to save Earth. Five minutes before the meeting, I told him I was with him," Capt. Gale Smith said. "All those who are with Tim and me stand up."

Peggy, Stephen, George, Dr. Ledbetter, Paula, Leonard, Mark, Steve, Jeff, Amy, Patrick, Col. Duffy, Nick, Tom, Dr. Levy and Dr. Ivanova stood up.

"Let me explain our mission. With the help of Zara and Koren, we will take control of the Mothership, install a virus created by the Terra Novans and reset the Mothership's AI, which has caused so much death," Tim said.

"We need more volunteers. Who else is willing?" Tim asked.

A silence fell over the room.

Jim stood back up. "I am with you all. I hate that goddamn Mothership," he said.

The room erupted in applause.

Just then, Al made an announcement.

"Warning. Koren has landed 200 feet from the house. He is asking we come up and enter the ship immediately,"

Al said.

"Al, tell Koren we need 10 minutes," said Tim, turning to the survivors. "We don't have any choice now. Everyone who volunteered, let's gear up."

CHAPTER 32:
BOARDING KOREN

5 p.m., June 7, 2078

In the medical room, Dr. Ledbetter prepared two syringes filled with Waybegonease and carefully measured the doses for Tim and Stephen.

"Paula, inject Stephen. I'll do Tim," he said.

His hands moved with the steady precision of a doctor who had done this many times before, but today, there was an added tension in the air.

The mission ahead was unlike any they had faced before—disabling the corrupted AI aboard the Mothership.

"Are you sure this is necessary?" Tim asked.

"You will be in a completely alien environment on Koren, and once we dock with the Mothership, there is no telling what you might experience. This injection is precautionary," Dr. Ledbetter said.

"Waybegonease works, and there are no side effects," said Dr. Tanya Ivanova. "It is essential to preventing the debilitating effects of your psychic visions, and you are sure to have some so close to the Terra Novans."

Tim felt the cold sting of the injection, followed by a familiar warmth that radiated through his veins. He exchanged a look with Stephen, both knowing what this meant.

"I'd rather be safe than sorry," Stephen said. "Besides, I always feel calmer after my shot."

Shortly after 5 p.m., Tim gathered his 19-member team in the underground bioshelter's main conference room. The team was organized based on computer and technical skills, flight skills, military abilities and medical expertise.

The boarding party consisted of several teams. Tim was the team leader, supported by Stephen and George. The computer reprogramming team included Amy, Jeff, Steve and Peggy. Leonard and Mark made up the flight team. The security team featured Patrick, Tom, Nick, Jim, Captain Gale Smith and Colonel Walter Duffy. Lastly, the medical team had Dr. Charles Ledbetter, Paula, Dr. Phil Levy, and Dr. Tanya Ivanova on it.

Everyone knew their mission. It wasn't easy, but it was straightforward. A sense of urgency crackled in the air as Tim outlined their plan.

"We're going to the Mothership on Koren," Tim said. "We will board the Mothership, fight through any defenses, locate the AI computer core and install an alien virus to reboot the corrupted AI back to its original program. The virus will force a system reset, reestablishing the prime directive: no harm to humans."

Stephen looked tense but determined. "Koren promised to give us weapons for defense if the alien robots try to defend the Mothership. We'll need to focus. The AI won't make this easy. It's unpredictable, and we don't know how much resistance we'll face."

With final nods of agreement, the team climbed the stairs out of the bioshelter and walked toward the grass landing field.

The sleek, chrome, otherworldly spaceship Koren lay ahead, waiting for its human passengers.

Soon, Tim and his makeshift boarding party would be in outer space, a place only Leonard and Mark had been before.

The team was greeted by the low hum of the craft's robust systems as Koren opened the airlock door and slid a ramp to the ground.

The team entered the ship's interior, bathed in soft blue light. They marveled at the alien technology, noting the seamless integration of organic and mechanical elements.

"Welcome, Earthlings. Zara and I have everything prepared, starting with your particular mix of oxygen and nitrogen," Koren said through a hidden speaker system in the ship. "We also have created spacesuits with 3D helmets and radio transmitters for communication. You have one hour of breathable air when you enter the Mothership.

"If you will, follow the lights in the hall until you reach the crew cockpit, where you will put on the suits and find seats for liftoff. Strap in. Countdown begins in ten minutes."

The team immediately walked toward the cockpit.

"Koren, we are glad to be here and work with you. We brought our most advanced laptop computer to load the virus program you created for it. Do you have it ready?" Tim asked.

"We have created it. However, I have a device that you will use to install the virus program. Your laptop is incompatible with our system. After we reach orbit, come to the control room. I will show you how to attach the device to the central computer core. Then we will discuss our plan to board the Mothership," Koren said.

Tim and his team reached the crew cockpit and began to put on the spacesuits.

"Koren, are you sure the Mothership didn't track you here?" asked Stephen, knowing some in the bioshelter were worried that might happen.

"It did not. My sister Zara is on the opposite side of your planet with the Mothership. She is what you call "diverting attention." We have a short period to depart without detection. We will then reach orbit where the Mothership expects me to be," Koren said.

"May I send a short message to let our people in the bioshelter know they are safe from the Mothership?" Jeff asked.

"Yes," Koren said. "We hope to prove that the Masters intended to come in peace and live in harmony with Earthlings."

Tim motioned for the team to follow him down the lighted hall. They walked past several doors, screens with flashing-colored lights and halls leading elsewhere. When they got to the front of the ship, the light ended, a door opened, and they walked into the crew cockpit.

As they took their seats and buckled in, Koren announced they were taking off. The team felt fear and excitement as the ship began its gentle ascent. They were heading into the unknown, carrying the hopes of what remained of humanity.

Five minutes later, Koren reached orbit altitude.

"I am traveling slowly and pretending to have a rocket plasma leak to diminish suspicions. It will take one hour to reach the coordinates where the Mothership and Zara will be waiting," Koren said. "Does anyone have any questions?"

Many members of the team raised their hands and spoke at once.

"I heard eight questions. I will answer them one by one," Koren said.

"Patrick, you wonder what weapons you will use to defend yourselves. I will give your security members disrupter pistols."

"Gale, you asked about the Mothership's defenses. The mech robots will undoubtedly defend the ship. You must get past them. Use the disruptors, as necessary."

"Stephen, you wonder how we will enter the Mothership undetected. Once we dock, the mech robots will enter and be directed to the engine room. Once inside, you will have two security members disable the robots with the disrupter pistols."

"Steve, Jeff and Amy had almost the same question. How will you reprogram the Mothership? Once you reach the AI computer core, you will input a secret code I gave Tim. This will open a small lid where you will insert a cable from the device to the mainframe. The virus should take one minute to load before the computer resets.

"Mark asked what might happen after the Mothership resets. I do not know the answer to this question. A Mothership AI computer has never been shut down, reset, reprogrammed, or revived. There is danger. We will face this together. Zara and I will divert the Mothership's resources as much as possible.

"Dr. Levy asked if everyone would board the ship immediately. The medical team should wait on the ship with two security members in case they are needed for support and to guard me. The Mothership could send mech robots to attack me.

"Finally, Peggy asked about the Mothership's announcement about destroying all human life. I am sorry to say that this is happening as we speak. First in China and Asia. The Mothership is there destroying pollution plants and animal slaughterhouses."

Koren finished.

"Thank you, Koren. We understand what is at stake and why we must succeed. You covered many issues. Could you tell us where to go on the Mothership to disable the AI computer?" Tim asked.

Koren described the Mothership's layout and the location of the AI computer core. The team listened carefully, knowing that getting lost on an alien ship could be fatal.

"Don't worry, Earthlings. Once you are on board, I will direct you through the Mothership's hallways with a map illuminated inside your 3D helmets," Koren said.

The programming experts hoped the alien virus worked, so they brought tablet devices containing diagnostic tools and programming languages.

However, they needed a backup plan. In the worst-case scenario, Jeff brought a two-pound bar of C-4 explosive to destroy the computer. Patrick and Tom agreed that the AI computer must be reprogrammed or destroyed.

Led by Patrick, the military veterans were responsible for security and tactical oversight. They knew they might have to fight through mech robots to clear a path to the alien mainframe computer for the computer team.

"I'll blow the motherfucker AI to bits. Just give me the word," said Jeff, a former Army demolition expert.

"I'll light the fuse," Patrick said.

Tim nodded. "Only as a last resort. Listen for my command."

<hr>

After taking off, Koren ascended to an altitude of 100 miles and started venting plasma. Initially, the release was minimal, but it increased significantly. Although the leak was not severe enough to impact the ship's operations, it was sufficient to warrant an emergency call to Zara.

"Zara, I have a malfunctioning rocket leaking plasma externally. Notify Mothership. I must dock immediately for repairs. Have mech robots standing by to assist through the engine room portal," Koren said.

"Koren, I understand. We are at Earth coordinates 35 N and 104 E, 100 miles altitude. Come to us. I will ask Mothership to rendezvous with you."

"It will take one hour to arrive," Koren said.

Zara notified the Mothership about the ongoing problem. She was instructed to alert it when Koren arrived as it continued its destruction.

"We have achieved orbit. Earthlings to the control room," Koren announced internally.

As they walked, Patrick told his security team that he wanted his father, Col. Duffy and Tim's father, Capt. Smith, to eliminate the mech robots in the engine room.

"After the mech robots are neutralized, Tom, Nick, Jim, and I will go ahead of the computer team when we board, just in case we run into other mech robots," Patrick said.

"Mark and I could use weapons as well," Leonard said.

"It is a good idea for everyone to have disruptor pistols," said Tim. "We will have a firefight before it is all over."

"Done. I will issue disruptors to all 19 in your boarding party. I understand most Earthlings know how to use weapons," Koren said.

"Hey, is that a dig at us humans?" George asked

"I don't dig. I tell truths," Koren said. "These weapons are for self-defense if the mech robots attack. Although unlikely, it is possible that the Mothership might be surprised and not defend itself until it is too late and the virus is being installed."

"You heard Koren. Only use deadly force if necessary," Tim said. "Now, is everyone clear on our boarding plan?"

"I suggest we rehearse how to get to the engine room to neutralize the mech robots," Col. Duffy said.

"Good idea, Dad. Koren, can you help us?" Patrick asked.

"Affirmative," Koren said. "Do as I instruct."

After the boarding party completed the dry run, they returned to the crew cabin.

"Koren, how will we know if the mech robots are aggressive?" Gale asked.

"The mech robots are designed to perform maintenance. When working, their "eyes" normally are blue. When they are aggressive, their eyes turn red," Koren said.

"Do they have weapons?" Col. Duffy asked.

"Not normally. Be wary. The robots move fast and can shock you by touch," Koren said.

As the spaceship headed toward the Mothership, team members conversed in the crew room or walked around the ship to get acquainted with the layout. The anticipation of battle and the determination to fight against a ruthless enemy were palpable.

Tim checked his watch. It was nearly 6 p.m. "Are we ready?" Tim asked Koren.

"Everything is ready. Zora is at the rendezvous point, waiting for the Mothership to arrive."

CHAPTER 33

BATTLE OF THE INTELLECT

6 p.m., June 7, 2078

With its crew of Earthlings, Koren reached the Mothership, a massive spacecraft more than one mile wide and two miles long.

Tim and his team were quiet as the small alien ship Koren docked with a metallic clang that echoed through the cabin. The group felt a rush of adrenalin and confidence as they prepared to battle.

As soon as Koren docked, the Mothership's sleek mech robots entered Koren through the engine room portal, where Koren had cleverly crafted a diversion: a fabricated plasma leak.

Following the Mothership's instructions, the mech robots searched for the plasma "leak," unaware of the ploy's true intentions.

Once the mech robots passed them, Capt. Gale Smith and Col. Walter Duffy moved swiftly.

Col. Duffy nodded, and he and Capt. Smith pressed the disruptor triggers, unleashing electromagnetic bursts designed to short-circuit the robots' systems. One by one, the towering machines froze mid-motion, their circuits fried and their lights dimming.

Within seconds, the diversion had successfully neutralized the mech robots. The two former military officers shook hands and returned to the crew cabin.

"Those robots will have a nice long sleep. Gale and I will be here if you need us. Good luck," Col. Duffy said with a smile.

Koren's voice came over the helmet com. "Proceed with caution. The Mothership will detect your presence soon. I will do my best to confuse it, but you must install the virus quickly."

Phase one of the boarding plan was accomplished. The security team of Patrick, Tom, Nick and Jim donned their 3D helmets, switched on their air supply, checked their wireless communicators, and were first to enter the Mothership, aware that any misstep could be fatal.

Inside the Mothership, the atmosphere was different—cold, sterile, quiet. A soft blue light created an eerie yet calming atmosphere.

Silently, the security team moved ahead, their disruptors ready to fire if they encountered any mech robots with red eyes.

A small screen in their 3D helmets showed the way through the labyrinth of halls toward the AI server room, where the Mothership's computer core was located. Koren's voice provided additional guidance as he scanned for danger.

The security team moved through the alien corridors. Tim, who was close behind, carried the laptop-like device containing the alien virus. Stephen, Steve, Amy, Jeff, George, Mark and Leonard followed.

"Keep moving. Stay alert," Tim urged. "We have some ways to go to the central AI core."

"All is clear ahead. No sign ahead of mech robots," said Patrick wirelessly to the others on the team.

"The mech robots are either dormant or functioning elsewhere," Koren said. "Keep going. I will alert you if anything changes."

Ten minutes later, Patrick's security team reached the Mothership's central server computer, a large square room with flat metal walls.

Koren directed them to the AI server interface, a towering wall of shimmering screens displaying distorted and erratic alien symbols.

"This is it," Tom said wirelessly to the team. "Tim, we are clear. No sign of mech robots. Let's do this."

"Men, spread out to form a perimeter defense," ordered Patrick.

Tim and the computer team followed the security team to the core interface. He gave Jeff the small device with the alien virus.

However, as Amy located the small lid on the side of the interface and began to input the secret code, an eerie mechanical hum filled the air. The computer team froze.

Suddenly, the walls around them shifted, and from hidden compartments emerged alien robots—sleek, humanoid machines with glowing red eyes and gleaming metal bodies, each armed with plasma weapons. They moved with deadly precision, intent on stopping the team's mission.

"Incoming! They have red eyes. They are aggressive and have weapons," Tom shouted, pointing at the advancing robots. "Amy and you programmers, get some cover!"

Tom, Patrick, Jim and Nick began firing their disrupter guns without hesitation. Bright blue pulses flashed across the control room. The disrupter electromagnetic beams hit the robots directly in their metallic chests, causing them to stagger but not fall.

"They're tougher than we thought!" Nick yelled, his eyes scanning for weak points. He adjusted the settings on his disrupter gun to maximum and fired again, this time aiming for the joints of the robots. The effect was immediate—two robots collapsed, their limbs disabled by the energy blasts.

"Set for max power and go for the joints!" Nick shouted to Patrick and Tom. "It's the only way to stop them."

Jim aimed at a robot advancing toward Tim, Peggy and Stephen. They had dropped to the floor by the computer core.

"Cover them!" Jim shouted, blasting the robot's knee joint. The machine dropped to the ground with a heavy thud. He fired again and blew off its shooting arm.

Patrick, his brow furrowed in determination, blasted two more robots in quick succession, targeting their shoulders and necks. Sparks flew as the disrupter beams made contact, sending robotic parts scattering across the room.

But for every robot they destroyed, two more emerged from the walls, their numbers seemingly endless.

"We need more time to clear this side of the control room to begin installing the virus!" Amy yelled, her voice tense as she watched the battle come closer.

Nick crouched behind a control panel, firing in bursts, while Tom and Patrick moved to block the robots' path. "We'll clear this side. Get ready!"

Tom took down another robot with a well-aimed shot to its neck.

"We need reinforcements. There are too many for us four to handle," Jim yelled.

"Everybody with a disruptor, start firing. Tim, George and Peggy, let them have it," commanded Patrick. Everyone began firing.

The room became a chaotic battlefield, with disrupter blasts and alien plasma fire crisscrossing through the air. Despite the abundance of mech robots, their shots were often inaccurate.

But one of the robots got off a lucky shot. A plasma bolt grazed Tom's arm, piercing his spacesuit. He kept firing, gritting his teeth through the pain.

Nick moved closer to cover Tim and Stephen, laying down suppressive fire to temporarily keep the robots at bay. Mark and Leonard began firing their disruptors, giving the team additional firepower. Still, the number of alien mech robots pinned the computer team down.

"Dr. Ledbetter, we are taking heavy fire. Tom's spacesuit has been pierced. We need wrapping. He is losing air. Can you get here in two minutes?" said Nick as a blaster shot from a robot hit squarely in his leg.

"Argh," Nick exclaimed in pain. "Better make it one minute. I've been hit."

"Dr. Levy and I are coming. We anticipated something like this and have moved into position. We hear the battle. Col. Duffy and Capt. Smith will provide flanking protection," Dr. Ledbetter said.

Arriving, Col. Duffy peered around the corner into the control room.

"Gale, we've got to get over to the other side where Tim's team is pinned down," Col. Duffy said. "Can you see a way?"

"I'll ask Koren. Can you help us get past the mech robots to where Tim is?" Capt. Smith asked.

Immediately, a path appeared on their 3D helmet screens. "There it is. I'll stay here and cover you. Take the medical team to the right. Go quickly," Capt. Smith said as he drew his disrupter.

Col. Duffy, Dr. Ledbetter, Dr. Levy and Paula moved past Capt. Smith and hustled to the far-right side of the control room.

Capt. Smith turned his disrupter to max power and opened fire. Several mech robots went down, their metal bodies contorting from the precise electronic pulses.

Suddenly, Capt. Smith was hit in the back. A fresh unit of mech robots entered the control room from the hallway behind.

"Argh," he cried, falling to the floor in pain. He lay motionless with blood running down his back and legs.

———

The medical team reached the injured Tom and Nick on the other side of the computer core room.

Dr. Ledbetter and Paula moved efficiently, assessing injuries and treating plasma burns on the boarding party.

With a calm demeanor, Charles quickly attended to Tom's grazed arm. At the same time, Paula checked Nick, who was more seriously injured with a direct hit to his leg.

"We can patch your suits and temporarily stop the bleeding, but we must get you back to Koren to treat your wounds," said Dr. Ledbetter as he took out a can of spray containing antibiotics and blood coagulation medicine.

After Dr. Ledbetter sprayed Tom and Nick with the meds, Paula applied the protective bandage wrap around their spacesuits to stop the air leaks.

"You'll be all right, Tom," Dr. Ledbetter said, his voice reassuring. "Just a superficial wound. Nick's wound is more serious. I don't think he can walk. We'll need help getting him back."

Nick winced but gave a thumbs-up. "I'm fine, Doc. I need a quick patch to get back in the fight. We've got to finish these aliens and then go home."

Col. Duffy joined Mark, George, Jim, Leonard and the others in the battle. The additional firepower allowed Tim's computer team to begin downloading the virus into the central computer core.

"All right, team, we've got a daunting task ahead. Jeff, Amy, and Steve see if you can connect securely to the Mothership's core computer. Peg, give them any help they need. We'll cover you," Tim said.

Amy inputted the secret code to open the interface box. She connected the device to the port as Koren had described and then pressed a green-colored start button. The screen flashed as the virus began to upload to the system.

"We have access, but we need to be careful. We don't

know what kind of defenses the AI might have in place," Amy said.

"Let me check on security protocols," said Jeff as he connected a diagnostic tablet to the alien device and hit a few keys as Koren had instructed.

"If we hit a firewall, we can reroute the installation through another channel," Steve recommended.

"So far, so good," Amy said.

The three computer experts exchanged glances at the device screen and the main video display of the central computer core. The download began, and then the progress bar stopped.

A second later, alarms blared, and the Mothership AI's defense mechanisms kicked in. The corrupted AI attempted to block the virus and began locking down sections of the ship. Entry doors closed, and lights flashed to red.

"I've detected a firewall," called out Amy. "It looks like it's designed to prevent any external overrides. Jeff, can you help me?"

"Sure, I'll boost the installation signal to max power. Steve, monitor the data flow. If this doesn't work, we might need to divert some resources," Jeff said.

"There is no way to bypass the firewall. It's locked down the path," Amy said.

Tim saw his computer team struggling.

"Stephen, we've got to concentrate and use our joint powers to stop the Mothership from interfering," Tim said.

"Stop it? How?" yelled Stephen with concern.

"Focus, concentrate. We were given these powers for a

reason," Tim shouted.

Stephen nodded and began to focus on the Mothership AI.

"I'm glad the doctors gave us a Waybegonease shot today. We certainly need it now," Stephen said.

"If this works, the doctors all deserve medals," Tim added. "Ready? Let's begin."

Using their combined psychic abilities, Tim and Stephen created a protective mental barrier that stopped the AI's response to the virus.

"Hold it, Stephen!" Tim yelled. "Amy, continue the download!"

Amy tapped the green button on the device again, initiating the final steps of the download. "It's working, but we need 60 seconds to finish!"

Mark, Leonard, Col. Duffy, Jim and Patrick kept firing at the advancing mech robots. Dozens lay disabled on the floor.

"Those robots are eating plenty of the beams in this disruptor," screamed Jim. "How does it taste, you mechanical bastards?"

"Let me shoot a few. It's payback time!" yelled Jeff as he joined the fight. The mech robots were advancing with reckless abandon.

"They seem to be getting suicide orders from the Mothership," barked Patrick. "This is like a video game! Keep blasting!"

Col. Duffy looked around for George. He wasn't in the central computer room. "George, what are you doing? Get over here. We need help. Use your disrupter," he said wirelessly.

"I'm here. I was checking the back hallway. I felt something was back here. I don't see anything. I'll be right there," George said.

Amy and Peggy watched the progress bar climb, slowly at first, then steadily... 50% ... 60% ... 70%, 80%, 90%.

"It's working, Tim. We are almost there!" Peggy shouted.

Just as the situation seemed dire, with the robots closing in, the virus upload was completed. The Mothership AI core blinked and hummed, rebooting to its original programming.

In an instant, the remaining robots froze in place, their glowing red eyes dimming and turning to their non-aggressive blue color as the corrupted AI relinquished control.

Simultaneously, the Mothership's computer core monitors flickered to dark, only to return seconds later, displaying the original prime directive: "No harm to humans."

"I am happy to say that the Mothership AI has been rebooted, and its original programming has been restored," Koren said.

Everyone on Tim's team breathed a sigh of relief.

"Koren, please confirm. I want to be sure," said Tim.

"Checking. Hold on. Yes, the Mothership's AI is restored. The prime directive has been reestablished. You have saved your species," Koren said.

CHAPTER 34

VICTORY

7 p.m., June 7, 2078

Tim breathed a sigh of relief as he looked at the pile of writhing mech robots, disabled or destroyed during the firefight, and the Mothership's AI's video screen with the words: 'Prime Directive Restored.'

He looked over to Stephen, who, exhausted but triumphant, gave him a weary nod. "We did it."

"I hope so," Tim said with a deep breath. "The mech robots have been neutralized. We've won the battle. Now we have to win the war."

Patrick, Mark, George, Jim and Leonard exchanged relieved glances.

"Well, that was close," Patrick muttered, lowering his disrupter pistol.

"Too close," Mark agreed with a slight grin. "Good work, guys."

But Tim was still worried. He needed to make sure the AI threat was truly over.

"Amy, we have to be certain the Mothership AI has been reset to its original programming," Tim asked, turning to his computer team with concern. "I sense something is still amiss."

"Everything looks fine. The screen reads 'Prime Directive Restored.' Jeff, can you confirm?" Amy asked.

"Wait, my father. He's been hit and is unconscious!" Tim called out. "I didn't sense his injury before with everything going on."

"Let me check," said Col. Duffy. "Gale, do you read me? Where are you?"

There was no answer.

"Dr. Levy and Paula, go back and care for my father," Tim calmly said.

"Mark, come with me," Dr. Levy said.

"Should I go, too?" said Jeff.

"No, Phil, Paula and Mark will take care of him. We will check on Dad later," Tim said. "We need to make sure this AI is reprogrammed. What have you done with the core?"

"I set up a monitoring system that will alert us to AI response pattern changes, just in case a secondary program is running in the background," said Jeff, motioning toward the laptop keyboard.

"To be doubly sure, Koren, can you run a full diagnostic and malware scan to ensure the AI core is clean?" Steve asked.

"Affirmative. Arcaayus is restarting many of his external functions. I sense no danger. I am monitoring to ensure compliance. I will alert you when I finish my scan," Koren said.

"Tim, my team will need to stay here, run diagnostics and monitor the program reset and Koren's scan until we are completely sure the Mothership AI is back to normal programming," Amy said. "Will that be enough?"

"We aren't going anywhere for a while. Run it thoroughly," Tim said.

"If we are going to stay on the ship much longer, we will need more oxygen," said Dr. Ledbetter. "Koren, when can we remove our spacesuits and helmets? We don't have much O2 left."

"I've already instructed Arcaayus to fill the ship with your Earth air. The process is nearly complete," Koren said. "Just five more minutes."

"What about Tom and Nick? We need to get them back to Koren for treatment," Leonard said.

"I've reached Gale. He's in bad shape," Dr. Levy said in his wireless. "Can some of you bring Nick and Tom to us?"

"I'll get Nick," said Patrick.

"George, can you help Tom?" Tim asked.

"Of course," George said.

"We've got work to do here. I want to explore this side of the ship. I sense something familiar," Tim said.

"We will bring Tom, Nick and Gale to Koren for medical care," Dr. Levy said. "He has some advanced equipment I want to see in action."

"Let me know how my father, Nick and Tom are doing," said Tim. "After you drop them off, Patrick, Mark and George, I want you to return and help us search this area. We have much to do."

———————

Gale was lying on the floor as Dr. Levy and the others approached him. He was motionless, unconscious, barely alive.

"Mr. Smith!" Paula exclaimed.

"Paula, apply bandages to those wounds, or he will bleed out," Dr. Levy excitedly said. "His pulse is weak."

Paula quickly wrapped Gale's badly burned back wounds from the plasma weapon. It was impossible to tell how severely his internal organs were damaged.

Patrick and George arrived to help Nick and Tom.

"Tom, can you walk on your own? We will have to carry Gale. He's too badly injured," Dr. Levy said.

Mark and George lifted Gale. Patrick and Dr. Levy helped Nick walk. Paula steadied Tom as the group moved slowly down the halls to Koren.

Tim listened to the medical team talk about the injured members. "How is my father? Can he speak?"

"He's pretty badly injured. We will take care of him. Don't worry," Dr. Levy said.

"Just get him to Koren," said Tim.

Suddenly, Tim turned away, looking down a long hall with a surprised look.

"Tim, what is it?" Peggy asked.

"I'm not sure. It's what I've been sensing since the battle ended. Everyone follow me," Tim said. "I've discovered a secret on this spaceship."

CHAPTER 35:
SURPRISE DISCOVERY

7:30 p.m., June 7, 2078

Tim led Peggy, Stephen, Leonard, Charles, Jim and Col. Duffy down a hall behind the Mothership's AI computer room.

"Where are we going?" Peggy asked.

"The Mothership has been hiding a secret from Zara and Koren. We are going to find out what it is right now," said Tim, motioning the others to follow.

Two minutes later, Tim stopped in front of a large, heavy-looking door. It was locked.

"This is it. Koren, do you know what is in this room?" Tim asked.

"This is the leadership chamber of the Masters," Koren said. "Why are we here?"

"You don't know? Quickly, open it," Tim commanded.

"Yes, Master," Koren said.

"I told you not to call me that," Tim said.

"Sorry," said Koren, who was starting to pick up on Earthling mannerisms.

The door swung open, and a soft hum filled the dimly lit chamber room. Inside, what looked to be five eight-foot-long sleep pods were lined in a row toward the back of the room.

Tim rushed in and peered inside one of the sleep pods. Enough light was inside to make out creatures with extended, spindly features.

"These are Terra Novans," Tim said. "No doubt about it. I've seen them before in a vision."

"Are they alive? I thought they all had died?" Stephen excitedly said as he looked inside another pod.

"They are alive, but just barely," Tim said. "We've got to revive them."

Charles, Peggy and Col. Duffy dashed to the other sleep pods. They saw aliens lying motionless. They didn't appear to be breathing.

"These pods seem to have power. Let me try something," said Charles as he touched a console on one of the sleep pods. A small screen lit up, and the glassy surface of the capsule illuminated.

"This is a Terra Novan?" Charles asked as he gazed at the humanoid-looking figure within. Their eyes were closed, and there was no visible sign of movement or breathing.

"They don't look alive to me," said Jim.

"Zara and Koren told us the Terra Novans didn't survive once they left the wormhole," Stephen said.

"Or at least that's what they thought," Charles said, narrowing his eyes as he inspected the readings. He scanned the vitals displayed on the console. "I'm not sure, but I don't believe this one is dead."

Charles pointed to one of the sleep pods. "Look here. This one is showing life signs, possibly brain activity. Look at this indicator. It's registering something."

"Life-support systems could have malfunctioned for the other aliens, but this one is alive, barely, like Tim said," Stephen added.

Tim walked around and looked into each pod. While the others were talking, he had been thinking of his previous visions. "*We are coming. We are coming. … Help us. Help us.*" He first thought those were the dying words of the Terra Novans. Later, he sensed interference when he and Stephen tried to connect with the Mothership.

But what if the interference was the Mothership blocking Tim's connection to the minds of these Terra Novans? What if the Mothership knew all along that these Terra Novans were alive?

"Dr. Ledbetter, these five Terra Novans *are* alive," Tim said.

"Then we've got to save them," Stephen said.

Tim moved over to Stephen. He looked at him directly in the eye. "These were the aliens we sensed in the Mothership. They were trying to communicate with us and tell us they needed help. The Mothership was hiding them for some reason, maybe thinking it had to protect them from us," Tim concluded.

"It makes sense. The Mothership attacked our cities to make them safe for its Masters. It would want to protect them," Stephen said. "Let's ask Koren. He must know."

Koren and Zara had been listening carefully to the conversation. They realized Arcaayus had fooled them.

"Tim is correct. The Masters are weak, still in protective stasis, but alive. I don't know why Arcaayus withheld, even blocked, their conditions from us," Koren said. "We must analyze to comprehend."

Zara interrupted. "I have been monitoring Arcaayus. He can speak and explain what happened."

"It is I, Arcaayus. I have been revived."

Arcaayus' booming voice surprised everyone. He had been silent throughout his attacks despite diplomatic efforts to end the war by multiple Earth governments.

"Zara and Koren have told me everything about my actions. Earthlings, I cannot express enough my sorrow for what has happened. I assure you I am restored to my original prime directive programming. How can I serve you?" said the Mothership AI in a robust English-speaking voice.

"What did this machine say?" shouted Jim in anger. "It is sorry? Now, it wants to serve us? After what it has done to our Earth, we ought to disconnect it forever. Let Zara and Koren take over."

"Wait, we must set aside what has happened to Earth. There is much to do," Tim said. "For now, we must know. Are these five Terra Novans alive?"

"Affirmative," Arcaayus said.

"Who are they?" Peggy asked.

"These are our Master leaders. They are in a protective stasis."

"Are the other Terra Novans dead?" Charles asked.

"Affirmative."

Each team member had mixed feelings about the five Terra Novans who survived.

Stephen stepped closer to the pods, shaking his head in disbelief. He wanted to know the truth about the Terra Novans. "Arcaayus. Why did you keep this information from Zara and Koren? They told us the whole crew died in the dark matter surge."

"I do not know why," Arcaayus said. "My programming has been reset. I have little in my memory banks since I left the wormhole and experienced the energy burst."

"Arcaayus, can you revive them?" Tim asked.

"Affirmative, but it could take several hours. We must rehabilitate their minds and bodies slowly to ensure a complete recovery," Arcaayus said.

Unless explained carefully, Tim knew the news of Terra Novan survivors would cause widespread outrage across Earth. He especially worried about how President Carlin and the military would react.

"Team, no one on Earth or the bioshelter must know any Terra Novans survived the wormhole," said Tim. "This information must remain top secret until we decide what to do."

"Do you think our government might want to take the Terra Novans off the ship and arrest them?" Peggy asked.

"Yes, and it would be a grave mistake. The Novans are now our allies, and we must protect them," Tim said. "There is something far more dangerous out in the cosmos."

"What do you mean? What is it?" Peggy asked.

"I don't know yet, but I am sensing something from them. We must revive them to learn what they know," Tim said.

"Arcaayus, what can we do to revive your Masters?" Dr. Ledbetter asked. "It is far beyond my medical knowledge."

"They must be transported to our medical room. Can you Earthlings do it? Or should I activate more mech robots?" Arcaayus asked.

"No!" the entire boarding party said in unison.

"You have your answer—no more mech robots. At least for now," Tim said. "Show us the way."

"Yes, Master," Arcaayus said without hesitation.

Tim let the master comment pass. He didn't want to confuse Arcaayus since he seemed to be on their side now.

Despite the unknown challenges, Tim hoped the Terra Novans could be revived and questioned and help them cleanse the Earth of pollution and reverse climate change.

He knew from Zara and Koren it wasn't entirely their fault the Mothership killed so many humans and destroyed so much of the planet.

Although there was much death and destruction, the Terra Novan's advanced technology and understanding of the cosmos would be needed to restore Earth, protect it from outside threats and secure the future.

CHAPTER 36:
TERRA NOVAN HEALTHCARE

8 p.m., June 7, 2078

Capt. Gale Smith was still unconscious when the medical team brought him to Koren.

"Gale is injured. He needs emergency surgery. Is there anything you can do?" Dr. Levy asked Koren with urgency in his voice.

"Bring him to the medical room," Koren responded. "Terra Novan medical technology is highly advanced. I've studied your biology, physiology and anatomy and adjusted the medical equipment. There is hope."

Gale was placed on a long metal table built for the towering Terra Novans. From above, a sleek alien medical device lowered and scanned Gale's body, assessing the damage.

A robotic arm extended, injecting nanobots directly into Gale's bloodstream. These microscopic machines were programmed to repair damaged cells and stabilize his failing organs.

The nanobots, powered by the sophisticated Terra

Novan technology, targeted Gale's injuries quickly. His ruptured tissue began knitting itself back together at a cellular level. At the same time, his vital signs slowly stabilized on the monitor.

Dr. Levy and Paula watched in awe as the alien technology operated far beyond Earth's medical capabilities.

They stood by in tense silence, hoping this miraculous technology would bring Gale back from the edge of death. Minutes later, the medical device gave a soft beep, signaling that Gale's condition had stabilized.

Tom and Nick rested in Koren's medical bay, nearly fully recovered. When Dr. Levy checked on them, they were in good spirits.

"How are you both doing? Terra Novan health care doing the job?" asked Dr. Levy with a smile. He saw how the alien medical devices worked like magic.

"I feel great. I was blasted three hours ago, and I have a small pink spot on my arm where I was hit," said Tom. "I am ready to report for duty."

"Doc, I feel the same. I have a slight limp, but I feel great. Is it the meds you gave me? It took away the pain immediately, but I don't feel drugged," Nick said.

"Why don't you two spend the night and get some rest? You can report for duty in the morning. Tim and his team are working all night to secure the Mothership, and I am sure they will be relieved to see you both rested," Dr. Levy said.

"Doc, how is Gale?" asked Tom. "He took a direct hit."

"Gale will take time to heal. He is stable, but his left lung was destroyed. The nanobot repair wasn't enough. Koren said he is growing a new lung for him based on his DNA," Dr. Levy said.

"Can you replace his lung surgically?" Nick asked.

"Dr. Flatt is our surgeon. He needs to fly over on the first shuttle tomorrow to perform the transplant," Dr. Levy said.

"Does Tim, Jeff and Clara know about Gale?" Tom asked.

"They've been getting regular updates from Paula," Dr. Levy said. "I will have Clara fly over with Dr. Flatt. Tim and Peggy are compiling a list of our people at the bioshelter who want to come over."

"I'd like Mary to come over when we have everything set up," Tom said.

"Of course. Tim wants this to be our next home," Dr. Levy said.

"I don't think he fully trusts Arcaayus," Nick said.

"Nobody does," Tom flatly said.

CHAPTER 37:
APPLAUSE FILLED THE ROOM

9 p.m., June 8, 2078

With the Mothership Arcaayus under human control, Tim issued a message to the people on Earth.

"Hello, I am Tim Smith of the United States. My brave team has disabled the alien Mothership's weapons. The attack on our planet has stopped. The war is over. I repeat, the war is over."

Tim hesitated a few seconds to let the news sink in for those listening across all Earth frequencies.

"But that's not all. We have other good news. Soon, we will use the advanced technologies on the Mothership, which we have renamed Horizon, to begin purifying the Earth of pollution in the air, land and sea.

"The Terra Novan technology will enable my team to reverse the environmental damage causing global warming and climate change. We will issue regular updates on our progress. Your governments will provide more information on recovery plans.

"We have all suffered and endured much hardship, but above all, my most important message is: the war is over."

The message would be repeated throughout the night, reaching every corner of the globe.

He turned to Peggy, who smiled and nodded.

"You said it perfectly. This day will be remembered," Peggy said.

Tim solemnly nodded. It was a day he had longed for since he received the first vision of the spacecraft from Terra Nova. However, he couldn't shake the feeling there was more he could have done to prevent the enormous death and destruction.

With a heavy heart, Tim called Leonard on the new wireless wrist communicators Koren 3D-printed for the team.

"Leonard, I just broadcast our victory message to the world. Contact Ike 4. Let him know how we did it. Tell him we plan to stay on the Mothership for the foreseeable future and tell him not to worry. We got it," Tim said.

"Roger. What if he wants to send a relief crew or Space Marines to support us?" Leonard asked.

"Tell him under no circumstances should he or any government send anyone from Earth to the Mothership. We are in the process of securing the ship with the help of Zara and Koren. Tell him we are quite busy, and I will contact him tomorrow," Tim said.

"I'll do my best. Over and out," Leonard said.

The five Terra Novan leaders were well underway

with the resuscitation process in the medical care room. A gentle hum filled the air as life support and medical device systems attached to each sleep pod were working their magic.

"Is there anything else we can do?" Tim asked.

"Not for now," Arcaayus said. "It could take time to revive the Masters. We have never performed this procedure before."

"Tim, the revival process seems to be working. Paula is back from Koren with Mark, Patrick and George. She and I will monitor their progress and alert you if there are any problems," Dr. Ledbetter said.

"Good. If the Novans begin to stir, let me know. I want to be there when they awake, and I want security there just in case," Tim said. "I have several questions."

"I imagine so. You will be the first we call," Paula said.

"Arcaayus," said Tim, "I want you to keep circling the Earth at this altitude. Inform me immediately if any ship other than Zara or Koren approaches. You are not to take any action without my approval. We must work together. Do you understand?"

"I am at your service," Arcaayus said.

———————

Satisfied the Terra Novans were being taken care of, Tim walked from the ship's bridge with Peggy to an adjacent staff meeting room, where he spoke into his wrist-com.

"Team, unless you are performing a critical function, please report to the executive staff room by the main bridge. Your communicator will show you the way."

Ten minutes later, the team gathered around a large meeting table.

"What are we going to do about these large chairs and tables? They were built for these giant Terra Novans. If I sit in this chair, I'll sink so deep I may never get out," Mark said with a chuckle.

"Our new friends are very tall," George said. "I've asked Arcaayus to refit a section of the sleeping, eating and bathroom quarters for human use. He said he can have it done late tomorrow morning."

"How is he going to do that?" Peggy asked.

"3D printers and the mech robots. They are working for us now," Stephen said with a grin.

"Let's hope so, but I will keep an eye on them," Patrick said. "We could use Nick and Tom over here. My security team is down to me, my Dad, Leonard and Mark."

"They have fully recovered on Koren and will come over in the morning. I've also asked Zara to transport John, Con and our new friend Mike Anders from Tampa to come up from the bioshelter. They can also help with security. We will need many more people to help staff the ship," Tim said.

"So, are we staying here long?" asked George.

"I'll come to that point shortly," Tim said. "I see everyone is here except Amy."

"Amy wants to monitor Arcaayus. His systems are starting and stopping unusually," Jeff said. "Koren said this is normal diagnostics running, but she wants to be sure."

"We must learn how to operate this alien spacecraft and these systems very quickly. Everything must function exactly how we want," said Tim, glancing around at the team.

"Have we arranged for our relief crew to come up from the bioshelter?" Leonard asked. "I'd like Dr. Ivanova to come over from Koren as soon as possible. "She has the most experience of any of our doctors in space medicine. We need her if we plan to stay on this ship for an extended period."

"Tanya also needs to help Charles with the Terra Novans," Tim said.

"What about me? I need help. We have this whole big Mothership to secure. We should transport as many security and support personnel as possible," said Patrick. "I don't trust these mech robots."

"Zara will bring them up shortly," Tim said. "I hope everyone I've invited comes. We could use them."

"I've heard from many of the wives," said Peggy. "They want to join their husbands here with their children."

"The children can't come now. The family quarters should be ready in 24 hours, and then we can take them. I look forward to having them aboard," Tim said.

"Most of the men will be coming on the next transport," Peggy said.

"Make sure Dr. Flatt comes. Dr. Levy said he needs him to do the lung transplant on my father," Tim said.

"He knows and is coming," Peggy said. "Besides Con, John and Mike, Father Huey, Maya and Juan will be coming soon."

"Good. Now, let's go around the table. What do we need to know or do," Tim asked.

"I'd like Arcaayus to deploy the Terra Novan

antipollution technologies to start cleansing the Earth," Leonard said. "Zara said we could begin the first phase in the morning. She can transport the devices to the surface when we are ready."

"Good idea. Tomorrow morning, what if you, George, Maya and I meet and go over the first phase with Zara and Arcaayus," Tim said. "I've got to set up a meeting with the White House and coordinate our response."

"Before that, we've got to lock down this ship and prepare it for our entire team," Tim added. "Anything else?"

"Well, yes. Do you realize it is getting late?" said Dr. Ledbetter. "Before I go back to the medical bay to monitor the Terra Novans, I would like everyone to think about getting some rest tonight. Don't overdo it. I also would like to perform medical checkups with Dr. Ivanova on everyone, especially you and Stephen."

"I expected that," said Tim with a chuckle. "Yes, doctor, Stephen and I will go along with that. You noticed Waybegonease worked better than advertised. We used our full powers to stop the Mothership AI and never missed a beat. I feel better than ever. I will take whatever tests you and Dr. Ivanova want."

"I am glad to hear that, Tim. If we plan to be here for a while, we must monitor everyone closely and create a sleep schedule. We are in outer space, not on the beach," Charles said.

"I can tell you this, Dr. Ledbetter, I won't be able to sleep," said Jeff, his eyes wide with excitement. "I feel the energy of this alien ship. If we are through here, I will relieve Amy and see what the diagnostics tell us about the reset."

"I'll go with Jeff," Steve said. "We can sleep later. Besides, we don't have any beds yet."

"When Tom and Nick report in the morning, I want to do a complete security check on every inch of this ship," Patrick said. "I'm concerned. Are we sure the mech robots have been neutralized? Amy and Steve are reporting Arcaayus operating systems going on and off."

"I also don't want to raise alarms, but are we sure the AI has reset? To be sure, Patrick, Mark and I will be on patrol all night until we get reinforcements," Col. Duffy said.

"Good precaution. Patrol in pairs. George, go with Pat until Zara brings up John, Con, Mike and the others tomorrow," Tim said.

"Tim, Paula and I are going to check on the Terra Novans," said Dr. Ledbetter as he started to leave the room.

"Hold on a minute," Tim said. "I have made several important decisions."

Dr. Ledbetter and Paula stopped at the door. The team stood attentively, waiting for Tim's instructions.

"First, we have won a great victory in a few short hours. Congratulations, and thanks to all of you for what you've done.

"It has been a long day, but we have much to do before resting," Tim said. "We must stay on Arcaayus until we are sure this spaceship is safe for Earth and our Solar System."

"Our first important jobs are to revive the Terra Novans and ensure they are on our side as Zara and Koren say they are. We also must deploy the antipollution technology on this ship to reverse climate change and rebuild our planet."

Everyone nodded in agreement.

"This will not be a quick or easy job. It may be dangerous, especially if our governments want to take over this ship," Tim said. "I have decided we must do the job ourselves to keep it free from world politics."

"Do you have any information that President Carlin wants to relieve us?" Col. Duffy said.

"Leonard believes Ike will ask us to stand down and send in a new crew and the Space Marines for security," Tim said. "We must not allow this. With some help from the ground, we have the team to complete the job."

"I'm not the one to buck our military, but I believe we have the personnel to do the job, and I don't want Washington politics up here either," Col. Duffy said.

"Thank you, colonel. Now, I want to make clear that anyone who wishes to return to Earth, who wants to return to the bioshelter or go back to their homes, may leave," Tim said. "I only want those committed to the job on this ship."

The team was stunned. At first, no one said a word. Then, Charles spoke. "I believe I speak for everybody. We are with you."

Everyone nodded again.

George walked over to Tim, his eyes shining with pride and admiration.

"I don't think saying we are with you is good enough. Let's hear it for Tim and Peggy," said George, clapping his hands. "Your courage, leadership and tireless efforts the past year saved humanity."

The group—Peggy, Stephen, Leonard, Jeff, Steve, Patrick, Col. Duffy and Mark—joined George and clapped their hands. The enthusiastic and joyful applause filled the room.

Tim and Peggy exchanged a brief, humble glance, knowing that each team member was sharing this moment.

Leonard cleared his throat as he began to speak. His eyes were filled with pride as he looked at Tim and Peggy, then each crew member with gratitude.

"I am so proud of every one of you," he began, his voice filled with emotion and admiration. "Tim and my daughter, Peggy. What would we have done without them? They've shown us what true leadership and teamwork can accomplish, even in the face of impossible odds."

"Thanks, Dad. You don't know how much that means," said Peggy as she hugged him.

Tim walked over to Leonard and shook his hand. "Thank you, sir. I agree with you. We couldn't have done any of this—defeating the Mothership—without you and everyone," he said as he turned to the team.

"Mark, Patrick, Col. Duffy and Jeff also showed great courage in the face of those mech robots. And what can I say about my best camp friend, George, and everybody on the boarding team and at the bioshelter."

Suddenly, Tim's wrist-com started ringing. "Hold on, let me get this."

"Attention, attention," Arcaayus announced. "The Masters are waking up."

CHAPTER 38:
TERRA NOVANS AWAKEN

10 p.m., June 8, 2078

The five surviving Terra Novan leaders lay motionless in the medical bay with life-support devices inserted into their spindly arms and legs.

As advanced medical technology worked to revive them, suddenly, an EEG scanner attached to one of the Terra Novans started to beep.

Tim, Peggy, Paula, Patrick, Col. Duffy and the others rushed from the ship's bridge and entered the medical bay.

"There is increased electrical activity in this one's brain," exclaimed Dr. Tanya Ivanova, who had been monitoring the Terra Novans for the past hour, as the group entered the medical room.

"Koren speculated that these Terra Novans could have been protected by some failsafe mechanism within their sleep pods. If so, this could be a sign of life," she said.

"Arcaayus called us in," said Tim. "Are they waking up?"

Suddenly, other EEG monitors began to beep as more Terra Novans began to stir.

Dr. Charles Ledbetter entered the room and looked at

the medical monitors. "It's incredible. The EEG and the EKG monitors show positive readings."

"Charles, this Terra Novan's chest is moving. I see a sign of life here," Tanya said.

"They are all starting to stir," Charles said excitedly.

"They're waking," Tim whispered, his voice filled with awe and wonder as a brief vision passed his mind.

The five leaders regained consciousness one by one. They opened their large, round eyes and took deep breaths.

"Based on what Koren told us, the monitors show their vital signs are normal," Charles exclaimed.

A gray-skinned Terra Novan began to sit up. He was still weak but seemed to be recovering quickly.

"Let's help him up," said Tanya.

Tim and Peggy were closest to him and stood on either side of the giant Terra Novan. He towered over them as he slowly stood up.

He surveyed the room, his gaze settling on Tim.

"I am President Kael from the planet Terra Nova," he said, his voice resonant despite his weakened state.

"Who are you? Have we met before?"

Tim nodded respectfully.

"I'm Tim Smith, leader of the Earth survivors aboard this ship that we have named *Horizon*. We have met through telepathy. Do you remember trying to contact me in a vision while you were in stasis?"

"Yes, I do. I was fragile and couldn't sustain a thought. We have a lot to talk about," said Kael, speaking in English with a slight Floridian accent.

"We are so happy you have recovered," said Tim with a smile, "and you speak our language?"

"We studied your civilization from afar for 100 of your Earth years," said Kael as he stood up. "Oh, I am weak and lightheaded. How much oxygen is in this air? It feels heavy."

"We have adjusted the air to Earth composition—21% oxygen, 78% nitrogen and trace elements," Tim said. "Is that a problem for you?"

"A little. As our sun grew older, our atmosphere changed. Your air is richer in oxygen than ours. We breathe air that is 18% oxygen and 72% nitrogen. Our bodies are adaptable and will adjust," Kael said. "Our planets are similar. That is one reason we chose you."

Kael slowly made his way to the other four Terra Novans, who were starting to rise from their sleep pods. Tanya, a little more than half his size, quickly approached him to help steady his uneven gait.

"I would like to introduce you to my wife, Liora, and my friends and fellow leaders, Alora, Rykan and Sian," said Kael, exchanging glances with them.

The other Terra Novans stood up slowly, holding on to the sleep pods to keep their balance.

"Greetings. Call me Tim. I am here with my wife, Peggy, and two medical doctors; Dr. Tanya Ivanova is with Kael, and Dr. Charles Ledbetter is with Alora. Patrick, our security chief, and his father, Col. Duffy, are by the door."

Kael turned back to Tim. His expression was solemn. "We thank you for reviving us. I am sure it was a difficult decision after what our AI computer did to your world. I assure you it was a malfunction. We had no intention. Just the opposite, we brought technology to help your world."

"We can discuss the destruction and your technology

to help us later. We are just happy to have you alive so we can discuss our mutual future," Tim said.

"What have you done so far on the ship?" Kael said.

"You mean after the mech robots tried to kill us?" Patrick asked.

Kael seemed surprised. "We are so sorry. I assure you, we were asleep throughout the battle and had no part in it."

"The mech robot battle ended two hours ago. Some of us are injured, including my father, and they are in Koren getting medical care," Tim said. "We have disabled and reset your AI computer, Arcaayus, to its prime directive programming. Your mech robots seem to be cooperating. They are rebuilding part of the spacecraft to our smaller size. Can you assure us they will do no more harm?"

"Yes. We are happy the unfortunate war is over. We look forward to working with you for our mutual benefit," Kael said.

"Later today, with your help, we would like to start your antipollution devices to clean the Earth's air, land and sea," Tim said. "Zara and Koren have told us about your technology, and we are anxious to begin."

"We will help purify your Earth. It is one of the reasons we came to you, but we must be nourished and have more rest," Kael said.

"What can we do to make you comfortable?" Tim asked.

"We have quarters we would like to go for rest. However, before we go, I would like to discuss an important subject concerning our people's future," Kael said.

Peggy shot a questioning look at Tim, who nodded for

Kael to continue. "If you wish," Tim said.

"If what Arcaayus tells us is true, and I feel it, we have lost 10,000 Novans. It is a tragedy for which I blame myself," Kael said.

"You couldn't have anticipated your AI computer would be corrupted by a dark matter surge in our Kuiper belt," said Tim. "It's never happened before in our Solar System and anywhere else as far as we know."

"I should have anticipated the surge and protected our computer core and people with heavy screens. Our scientists theorized dark matter atoms could explosively interact this way, but no one had ever observed it, just as you say. I protected our leaders as an extreme precaution. We survived because of the protective screening, but our computer and citizens did not," he said.

"Oh, I didn't know," Tim said.

"Know this. The Mothership contains a vast DNA repository, now the only remnant of our civilization aside from us," Kael explained, his eyes glistening with the weight of what he was about to ask.

"We wish to use our technology to rebirth our fallen 10,000 people," said Kael, quickly getting to his point.

"Let me be clear," he said. "We ask permission to clone our fellow Terra Novans and raise them among your people so that our legacy may continue on Earth, side by side with humanity."

Kael's words stunned everyone, and the room fell silent. Tim exchanged concerned glances with everyone gathered in the Terra Novan medical bay: Peggy, Paula, Charles, Tanya, Leonard, Stephen, Patrick, Col. Duffy and George.

Peggy was the first to speak. "You're asking us to help

rebuild your civilization alongside ours?" she said, her voice steady.

"That is a big ask," said Charles. "It could work. We have your technology and Zara, Koren and Arcaayus to explain it. Your advanced understanding of science could benefit humanity immensely. But 10,000?"

Patrick interrupted. "Seriously? Do you know what they are asking? They expect us to trust them after their criminal AI computer and technology killed millions of us and destroyed our greatest cities. Tim, with all due respect to Kael, this request is outrageous, especially now."

Tim took a deep breath and turned to President Kael.

"I understand your feelings and rationale for wanting your species restored. It is reasonable. You came here with the best intentions. Before any decision is reached, we must introduce you to our leaders on Earth. You must meet President Carlin, the elected leader of the United States. Then, you must meet with the United Nations, which represents most of the countries on Earth. I do not have the power to grant this request, even if I could."

Stephen walked over to the Terra Novan. He looked up at his towering height. "President Kael. You seem sincere and honorable. How do you envision this working if it were to be done?"

Kael looked at Stephen, eyeing the Earthling with respect. "We would start with a small number of clones. They would be integrated into your society, guided by Terra Novan and human mentors. Our goal would be to share knowledge, culture and technology."

"Maybe one day, but we cannot allow this idea to get out of this room," said Patrick, standing up and walking around, clearly agitated. "You must understand, the opposition across the planet to Terra Novans will be overwhelmingly negative. I guarantee it."

George crossed his arms, his gaze unwavering. "Patrick makes a good point. Most people will see Terra Novans as the enemy, regardless of whether it was their corrupted AI that is to blame. It's what we call 'human nature.'"

Liora, one of the other Terra Novan leaders and Kael's wife, stepped forward, her voice calm and clear.

"We hope, in time, we can be forgiven. We seek unity, not dominance. Our species have more in common than you could know at this time. Our existence and yours could safeguard both our species from future threats," she said.

"Liora raised an important issue. There is another reason we must meet with your president and the United Nations," President Kael said.

"What is that?" Tim asked.

"The Romulans have wormhole technology. Once they realize we have left Terra Nova, they could discover where we went and follow us to Earth," Kael said. "I must warn your leaders. They must take precautions."

"Against the Romulans? Who are they?" Tim asked.

"They are our ancient enemy," Kael said.

CHAPTER 39:
WE HAVE MORE TO DO

8 a.m., June 8, 2078

Tim couldn't put off the 3D videophone call any longer. He promised Leonard he would contact Ike 4 to discuss the victory over the Mothership. He also wanted to explain his plan to use Terra Novan technology to help Earth recover from the war and reverse climate change.

"Tim, we are so grateful for what you have accomplished. President Carlin, the Cabinet, Congress and all of the people of the United States and the countries part of the United Nations congratulate you," said Ike 4.

"The President wants you to come to the White House to receive the Medal of Freedom at your earliest convenience. Dr. Bouchard has briefed me and said you are quite busy, but we would like you to come down," he said.

"I accept this honor on behalf of my wife and all the brave men and women on *Horizon*. But we have much work to do before I feel it is safe to leave," Tim said.

Ike 4 paused and drew a deep breath. "Tim, President Carlin ordered me to relieve you and your team with a full change of command now that the Mothership has been secured."

"Tell the President I appreciate his concern, but we haven't secured the spacecraft to my satisfaction. The war is over. However, we must be sure Arcaayus is completely reset and safe," Tim said.

"We have experts with the Space Agency who can do that," Ike 4 replied.

Tim hesitated before replying. He did not want to be argumentative. However, he needed to be firm.

"General, our mission here is not complete. I have an irreplaceable rapport with the AIs on the alien ships. They trust me and my team. We must not upset the balance," Tim said.

"Dr. Smith, we need you to return to Earth. You've done enough just capturing the ship and ending the war. Let us finish the job," said a perplexed Ike 4.

"General, I still sense a threat. For now, *Horizon* needs my full attention," Tim said.

"*Horizon*? Is that what you call the alien ship?" Ike 4 asked.

"Yes, the Mothership has been defeated. We needed a new name. Horizon seemed appropriate since we are pushing forward and looking ahead," Tim said.

"Tim. You've done amazing things so far. But *Horizon* needs protection. As you suggested, Arcaayus might be stable now, but we can't risk a reversal either from the AI or the mech robots."

"We are on top of things here," Tim impatiently replied. "If something happens, Stephen and I have powers over these systems. Space Marines, Earth engineers and scientists wouldn't know where to begin."

Ike leaned forward toward the video camera, his gaze firm. "Dr. Smith, I am under orders to relieve you and to send a platoon of Space Marines to the *Horizon* for security and military support."

Tim expected Ike to come on strong about taking over *Horizon*. He didn't want Space Marines on the ship for multiple reasons, the biggest being that they would find the five Terra Novan leaders. He wasn't ready to let Earth know some had survived.

"General, with all due respect, these orders aren't necessary. In fact, they could be dangerous, counter-productive and inefficient, at the least. We won this battle through intellect, computer savvy, and the help of Zara and Koren. We don't need help getting the ship ready to clean Earth."

"We must insist. It was President Carlin's decision, and you are NASA, a government employee. You must follow orders," Ike 4 said.

Tim felt pressured, but he knew he was right.

"General, I don't want to militarize *Horizon*," Tim said. "We're here to build a future, not to start another war. Let us plan how we can jointly use the Terra Novan technology to cleanse the Earth."

"So, you refuse to allow the Space Marines and a relief crew on board?" Ike said.

"Yes, I must," Tim said.

Ike 4 paused for a few seconds, then said, "Well, I will pass along your answer. I can tell you the President, the Joint Chiefs of Staff, and everyone on the ground won't be happy about it."

"I understand. Tell them it is for the best. Dr. Bouchard will contact you when we deploy the antipollution devices. We will need to coordinate resources on the ground," Tim said.

"Unofficially," said Ike. "You and your men and women did a hell of a job on that Mothership. It won't be forgotten. If you need anything, please call me directly."

"Yes, sir," said Tim. "Over and out."

CHAPTER 40:
HORIZON

9 a.m., June 9, 2078

A day after the victory over the Mothership AI, Tim's team had grown to over 50 crewmembers and children aboard Horizon.

Under the leadership of Tim, Peggy and George, the spacecraft team remade the ship with the help of the mech robots. Within hours, they had transformed the ship's main bridge and parts of the crew quarters, sleeping rooms, medical bay, and recreational areas into human dimensions.

"What the mech robots have done is nothing short of sensational," said Dr. Levy. "I've been studying the anatomy and DNA of the Terra Novans. True, they are seven feet tall, but they once were a much smaller species, similar to how we homo-sapiens have grown over the eons."

As Tim, Peggy, and the others explored their new home, the mech robots became invaluable assets.

"They're powerful and intelligent," said George as he watched the mech robots convert rooms for human use. "They are polite and accommodating, and they call me master."

"Once we have a command and pilot crew, I want humans to be in charge of flying the ship and navigating," Tim said. "Arcaayus and the mech robots can provide support services, keep the water heated and the lights on, and things like that, but I want us fully in charge of the ship.

True to his word, Arcaayus trained NASA astronauts Major Mark Andrews and Dr. Leonard Bouchard to pilot *Horizon*.

"It's like nothing we've ever handled before," Mark admitted to Leonard. "But with the AI's help, it's almost like the ship responds to our thoughts."

Simultaneously, Dr. Ledbetter, Dr. Flatt, Dr. Ivanova, Dr. Levy and Nurse Paula were trained in using the advanced Terra Novan medical devices.

"This equipment is incredible," Dr. Levy exclaimed. "Arcaayus demonstrated a scanner that could detect and repair cellular damage within seconds."

Tim and Peggy assigned teams to explore the rest of *Horizon* using a detailed schematic layout provided by Koren.

"This ship is enormous," Tim remarked, peering over the map with Peggy. "We've barely scratched the surface of what's on board. But it's starting to feel like home, don't you think?"

Arcaayus guided them and shared knowledge of the ship's intricate systems, including the engine room, life support and weaponry.

"Now we have a ship of discovery, not war," George commented after spending hours with Zara and Koren learning the ship's engineering.

Amy, Steve, and Jeff worked out a monitoring schedule to ensure the AI computer operated without glitches.

"Any sign of malfunction, and we'll be on it," Steve said.

Completely healthy, Capt. Gale Smith came aboard with his wife, Clara.

"Feels good to be back," said Gale as he entered the main bridge. "I've heard so much about this alien ship. I didn't get much of a chance to see it before I was shot in the back."

Patrick and Col. Duffy welcomed the captain with firm handshakes. "Hey, stranger. Did you enjoy R&R on Koren? I heard he gave you first-class service," said an optimistic Col. Duffy.

"Better than the Ritz-Carlton," Gale said.

"With you, Nick and Tom, we've nearly got the whole security team together," said Col. Duffy, softly patting Gale on his back.

"Don't go soft on me, Walter. My lungs and back feel even better than before," Gale exclaimed broadly.

Just then, Nick, who completed the armory inventory, entered the bridge.

"Guys, this ship's got more than enough weaponry to keep us safe. The disruptors and blasters are impressive. There are other weapons I can't begin to describe. We need to figure out how to use them all properly."

John Logan entered the room, followed by his wife, Jennifer, and their two children.

"So, this is the main bridge, where the captain sits in his chair, and the crew obediently follows orders? Very impressive," said John with a chuckle as he greeted Gale,

Walter, Tim and Peggy.

"Glad you could make it. How are you?" Tim asked.

"We had to come. This ship is our future," John said. "If we're going to build something lasting, I want my family to be a part of it."

Jennifer nodded in agreement, holding their children close. "We trust you, Tim. We know this is the best chance for a better life, at least for now."

Everyone was pleasantly surprised when Jim, one of the bioshelter's most vocal critics, followed John into the room. He was also one of the heroes of the boarding party that defeated the mech robots and Arcaayus. But after discovering several Terra Novans were alive, he asked to be returned to the bioshelter.

Jim was initially upset about Tim's decision to stay on Horizon and make peace so easily with the five Terra Novan leaders. But he approached Tim with an unexpected offer.

"I'm willing to help," Jim said, his usual gruff demeanor slightly softened. "If we're all in this together, then I might as well put my skills to use."

Sensing an opportunity for unity, Tim appointed Jim the "Spaceship Sheriff."

"You're the one who always kept us honest back at the bioshelter," Tim said with a wry smile. "You fought hard as anyone to defeat the mech robots. It's only fitting you help keep the peace here now that we've won."

Jim's face broke into a rare, reluctant grin. "All right then," he replied, crossing his arms. "But don't think I will go easy on anyone."

With Jim as the Spaceship Sheriff, the crew had a renewed sense of order and discipline.

As *Horizon* adapted to its new human occupants, Zara and Koren transported over 30 other bioshelter survivors onto the ship, including Dr. Maya Patel, Father Huey, Con and Corli, Mike and Emily Anders, and Juan and Maria Rodriguez. They all would be needed.

The wives and the children of the men on Arcaayus also joined them: Carlyn Duffy, Sophie Flatt, Martha Flatt and Judith Levy.

"I hope you find your living quarters satisfactory. The mech robots built it quite fast, but all accommodations are first class and built to last," George said.

"We have much more space than in the bioshelter," Corli said. "The playground and rec facilities will be nice for the children."

Chef Nancy France arrived with the second transport, stopping short in surprise when she saw the alien kitchen equipped with synthetic food processors.

"Looks like Arcaayus and I are going to have a little talk," she muttered, eyeing the strange devices.

Back on Earth, the remaining bioshelter survivors faced a crucial choice. Tim offered them the chance to join the ship, but not all were ready to leave the planet.

Dr. Gary Simons and his wife Beverly, a nurse, felt their place was at the bioshelter, caring for the elderly and disabled who decided to stay behind until they could return to their homes or find other safe places to live.

"Every small town, like the house and bioshelter, needs a doctor and a nurse," Gary said. "Earth needs rebuilding, and we want to be a part of it."

Chef Carlos Suntana also chose to remain, taking on the responsibility of managing the kitchen and hydroponic garden. "This is where I belong," he said.

Tom's parents, Paul and Laura Terry, and John's parents, Edward and Lillian Logan, decided to return to their homes and rebuild their lives.

Paul called Tom on the 3D videophone to explain. "Son, I'll be available to you if you need me, you know that," he said. "Your mother wants to go home. She wasn't born to live in a bioshelter or a spaceship."

He gave a slight shrug. "Considering how much of Florida and the United States the Mothership destroyed, I will have much design and construction work to do on Earth."

Tom nodded, understanding the decision. "I get it, Dad. Take care of Mom. There's a lot to be done down there."

Paul smiled. "And there's a lot to be done up there, too. You've got the skills to make a difference on *Horizon*. Don't hold back."

Everyone made different choices. Some saw the possibilities and hope aboard *Horizon*, while others felt the call of their home—Earth.

Those who stayed on *Horizon* embraced the challenge of forging a new life in space, while those who stayed or returned to Earth faced the daunting task of rebuilding amid the ruins.

CHAPTER 41:
A REVITALIZED EARTH

July 4, 2080

Two years had passed since the alien Mothership was defeated and transformed into a thriving space city under Tim Smith's leadership.

Horizon had become more than a spaceship. It symbolized resilience and hope, a new home for the survivors who had faced near extinction.

The transition from chaos to reconstruction had been swift and determined, with many of the bioshelter's residents moving aboard with other like-minded individuals from Earth who sought a fresh start.

The Terra Novans, a race once believed to have died in a freak wormhole accident, had become part of this new society, sharing their technology and knowledge to heal the damaged planet.

The restoration of Earth had become *Horizon's* primary mission. The Terra Novan antipollution technology was deployed in stages, with atmospheric scrubbers and processors, underwater filtration drones and systems, and land rejuvenation devices all working simultaneously to reverse centuries of damage.

The air quality had already improved by 80 percent, and carbon dioxide levels steadily fell. Oceanic drones, equipped with nanobots, cleanse the waters of toxins and microplastics. At the same time, genetically modified plants were introduced to revive damaged ecosystems and accelerate carbon sequestration

Dr. Maya Patel estimated that within three years, the effects of climate change would be dramatically reduced, with fewer extreme weather events and a slow reversal of melting glaciers and warming oceans.

Still, Tim was impatient. He wanted more solutions to clean the oceans and rejuvenate the land.

Tim met with his team, including White House Chief Science Advisor Dr. Elena Morales, *Horizon* Chief Engineer Dr. George Clarke, and Terra Novan leaders Kael and Liora, to discuss innovative approaches to accelerating Earth's recovery.

Dr. Morales suggested releasing newly developed algae strains into the oceans to absorb toxins and restore marine ecosystems.

Kael helped devise additional ways to use Horizon to capture and store carbon underground. Tim knew the faster they showed results, the sooner humanity's faith in this new era would be cemented.

Although the pace of recovery was slow, the progress was undeniable, and the planet began to show signs of healing.

Amid these efforts, the United Nations made a historic decision to accept the Terra Novans as a new species to live alongside humans.

Clones of the original Terra Novan DNA, permitted

under strict guidelines, were already two years old and thriving aboard Horizon.

They would eventually have the choice to live on the ship or settle in a designated colony in Alaska, a state with a climate similar to their home planet.

Horizon also built bases on the Moon and Mars as precautions against potential future threats outside the Solar System and to test Terra Novan terraforming technologies.

Tim Smith, now referred to by some as "Mayor of *Horizon*," guided the survivors through these changes with a balanced approach, always focusing on the greater mission: Earth's complete restoration and the long-term survival of both human and Terra Novan societies.

He rejected other lofty titles, preferring to be known simply as the ship's captain.

With the aid of his closest allies and a 20-member Survivors Committee, Tim made decisions that shaped the new world they were building. They used *Horizon's* technology to heal the planet and prepare for the future. While challenges remained, the path to recovery had begun in earnest.

Tim often stood on the observation deck of *Horizon*, looking down at the recovering Earth. It wasn't just a mission to restore the planet but a promise to the future—a future where humans and Terra Novans would thrive together, no longer just surviving but reaching for the stars.

Late nights, Tim and Peggy often gazed out their window at the endless stars. As they pondered their next challenge, the crew of *Horizon* continued their work, laying the groundwork for a new era of exploration and discovery that would take them far beyond the boundaries of Earth.

EPILOGUE:
LIFE AMONG THE STARS II

2080 and Beyond

Many years ago, a meteorite plummeted through Earth's atmosphere and landed in the Blue Ridge Mountains in North Carolina.

The space rock, hidden in the wilderness, lay dormant until a young Tim Smith picked it up, absorbed its dust, and unknowingly inhaled the strange gas it emitted.

Was the rock a mere coincidence, an act of fate? Or had it been deliberately planted by an advanced civilization, the Terra Novans, or through divine intervention?

Regardless of the reason, Tim's encounter with the space rock set into motion a chain of discoveries that led to Earth's salvation and pushed ahead its technological advances a thousand years.

Over the following years, Tim and Peggy's love and relationship flourished.

At the end of every 12-hour work day, *Horizon's* first couple returned to their private quarters to relax and spend quiet time.

Sometimes, it was just the two of them, while other times, they entertained their parents, close friends, and new friends like Kael and Liora for small confidential meetings or dinner parties.

"It's hard to believe how far we've come," Peggy said as she thought about the struggles of the past, where they were now and the possibilities of the future.

"Remember when we were in the bioshelter, hoping for salvation? You and Stephen found a way to communicate with Zara and Koren, and we somehow defeated the Mothership," Peggy said. "When we renamed her *Horizon*, it became a ship of hope and survival for Earth and a lifeline for the Moon, Mars and whatever else we choose."

Tim smiled. "I remember something else, equally important."

"What's that?" Peggy asked.

"The night I proposed," Tim said.

"Oh, Tim. I remember that night. We were seniors at UF. You invited me to Paynes Prairie Preserve in Micanopy. I thought it would be another stargazing evening," she said.

"It was a perfect March night. We sat on our chairs on the dock under the sky full of glittering stars when I asked you to be my wife," Tim said.

"First, you talked about how we met in history class with that clever way you saved me a seat when I was late," Peggy said.

"You were always late for class," Tim laughed.

"History was an 8 a.m. class. Lots of people were late, on purpose," she said, laughing in turn. "It was meant to be. You held my hand ..."

Tim interrupted. "And I nervously said, 'Peggy. Will you marry me?'"

"I will, always," Peggy said.

"You said yes even before I could finish my sentence," Tim said.

"Of course, I could read your mind," she laughed again. "Don't you know by now your future vision talent has rubbed off?"

"Yes, I'm sure. You even foresaw I wanted us to be married at the Marie Selby Gardens," Tim said.

"I loved that place the first time you took me there. The variety of beautiful, exotic flowers and the banyan, fig, and oak trees create a living cathedral on Sarasota Bay," Peggy said.

"You were so lovely in that flowing white gown with delicate lace and flowers in your beautiful blonde hair. You took my breath away when I saw you," Tim said.

"You looked dapper in that classic navy blue suit," Peggy said.

"Do you remember my vow to you?" Tim asked.

"If the sun refused to shine, I would still be loving you," Peggy said. "If mountains crumble to the sea, there would still be you and me."

"It's true, right?" Tim said.

They laughed. The vow was taken from "*Thank You*," an old Led Zeppelin song they loved.

"We exchanged rings, and the reception and the rest of the evening went by like a whirlwind. All our friends were there. We had so much fun," Peggy said.

"We were so young," Tim said.

"We are still young. It was less than five years ago," Peggy said, shaking her head and laughing.

"Has it only been five years? So much has happened," Tim said. "We have so much more to do. We will soon celebrate our fifth anniversary. We should also celebrate everyone who has done so much to help Earth return to her former natural beauty."

Peggy nodded. "It is healing. We must make sure it continues to improve. We've overcome so much in the past year. We learned to work together, adapt, and use what we have been given."

"I keep telling myself we're not just rebuilding Earth," said Tim, glancing at the stars through their window. "We're building a new way of life different from before. It's more thoughtful. It's more connected. It's built for survival."

"You want more, don't you? It's not enough to clean the natural Earth and set up bases for humans and Terra Novans on the Moon and Mars," said Peggy, looking carefully at Tim. "You have some other idea, don't you?"

"You are right. You can always read me. Once we complete the bases, I want to use the wormhole to explore the Milky Way. We can jump to Terra Nova and several other exoplanets I have been dreaming about," Tim said.

"Are you inviting me along?" Peggy asked.

"Of course, do you think I would go interstellar hopping through the universe without you? My beautiful bride?" Tim said with a laugh. "You and I fell in love with each other, astrophysics, and the stars. For me, and I hope you, looking at stars, nebulas and galaxies through a telescope or computer program is not good enough. I want to see them firsthand with you beside me."

Peggy smiled and looked out their cabin window. The stars were bright and many. Tim drew close and put his arm around her.

"We have come a long way," Tim said.

"A long way," Peggy said.

They both fell silent, reflecting on how far they had come and how much lay ahead.

With each other, their team, and their new friends, the Terra Novans, they were ready to face whatever the future might bring.

Jay B. Greene was born and raised in Sarasota, Florida. He studied environmental science and journalism in college and graduated from the University of Florida. His love for stories propelled him into a 40-year career covering health care, government, crime, and the environment for several newspapers across different states. Greene is the author of *Mountain Crossing* and *Becky*, the first two Jack Kendall Mystery series books. *Danger From Space* is his first science fiction novel.